JACQUIE D'ALESSANDRO
Why Not Tonight?

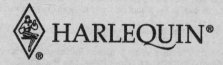

HARLEQUIN®

TORONTO • NEW YORK • LONDON
AMSTERDAM • PARIS • SYDNEY • HAMBURG
STOCKHOLM • ATHENS • TOKYO • MILAN • MADRID
PRAGUE • WARSAW • BUDAPEST • AUCKLAND

This book is dedicated with my love and gratitude to my incredible husband, Joe, whose unfailing support humbles me and who never tires of saying, "You can do it"—no matter how many times a day I need to hear it. And to my wonderful son Chris, for being so much like his dad.

Acknowledgments

I would like to thank the following people for their help and support: Brenda Chin, Damaris Rowland, Ernie Sigismondi, JoBeth Beard, Wendy Etherington, Jenni Grizzle, Kay and Jim Johnson, and Lea and Art D'Alessandro.

ISBN 0-373-79204-2

WHY NOT TONIGHT?

Copyright © 2005 by Jacquie D'Alessandro.

www.eHarlequin.com

Printed in U.S.A.

1

One week before the blackout

ADAM CLAYTON LOOKED around the photo studio and asked himself what the devil he was doing. It was one thing to help out Nick with paperwork while his buddy was at the hospital about to become a new dad, but there was no way Adam could actually take the photos for the appointments booked into Nick's studio today. He was a stockbroker, not a photographer. Or at least he used to be a stockbroker. Now he was a…

He dragged his hands through his hair. What exactly *was* he? Career-wise, he didn't know, and it had become increasingly clear to him every day since leaving Wall Street two months ago that, while he'd accomplished his goal of minimizing the health-threatening stress in his life, he didn't like not knowing what he was. Who he was. Where his life was heading. For a guy who'd always defined himself by his career, he now felt like a ship without a port.

He frowned. Surely this disquiet was only temporary. He just needed more time to get used to being out of the rat race. Still, it was difficult for him not to have a grasp on things. He'd always been so disciplined, his schedule so regimented, his time so consumed with work, that he was finding it a real challenge to take it easy.

He missed the passion and energy his hectic, frenetic work had inspired. He needed to find another outlet for that energy and passion—something that would bring him the same sense of satisfaction but wouldn't make him face another health scare like the one he'd recently experienced. Nothing quite as sobering as a grim-faced cardiologist asking him if he wanted to end up like his father. Which he sure as hell did not. Lying on that gurney, with all those monitors beeping around him, had been a major wake-up call. He'd realized then and there that he needed to change his life—*now*. Not at some nebulous point in the future. So, two weeks after those chest pains had landed him in the emergency room, one month after his thirtieth birthday, he'd officially "retired" from Wall Street. He had no intention of becoming a statistic and leaving behind a young wife and family like his workaholic, stockbroker father had.

Now, with nothing and no one to worry about except himself, he was finally free to do some of the things he'd always wanted. Things he'd never had the time to do. Top of the list—three months in Europe. During college, he'd twice planned to spend the summer trekking around Europe, but on both occasions his plans had been thwarted. First time courtesy of illness. Talk about a lousy time to catch mono. Second time…

He blew out a deep breath and forced back the barrage of memories that threatened to sneak out of the place where he kept them carefully locked away. Second time he'd cancelled because he'd fallen wildly, passionately in love and hadn't wanted to spend one minute, let alone the entire summer, away from her.

He shook his head to dispel the image that rose in his mind's eye of the laughing, smiling girl who'd so thoroughly captured his heart that long-ago summer. His gaze fell upon the photo on Nick's desk—an eight-by-ten of a smiling Nick and Annie on their wedding day two years ago—and a wave of undeniable envy washed through Adam. Maybe he didn't know what sort of new career he wanted, but one thing he definitely did know—he wanted the kind of loving, happy relationship Nick and Annie shared. The same kind his parents had shared…until his father's death.

But not just yet.

No, first he planned to enjoy this time off—the first he'd had in years, and indulge in his lifelong dream of seeing the world—at something less than warp speed. Except for the Caribbean, he'd never traveled outside the United States. And he'd never been anywhere for more than three days at a time. Growing up, his family's vacations had consisted of quick jaunts over two- or three-day weekends when the stock exchange was closed. Due to the Clayton family vacation time constraints, the rule was their destination couldn't require more than a three-hour flight or a four-hour drive.

Since he was a kid, he'd always wanted to go somewhere far away and stay there for more than thirty-six hours. Bask in the culture, take his time to explore the intricacies of a single city. As of yet, it hadn't hap-

pened. With his crazy work schedule, he hadn't taken
a vacation of any length in more than five years. Now
he had his chance and nothing was going to stop him
from snatching the brass ring he'd waited so long to
grab.

Yet, except for his travel plans, he hadn't made any
definite decisions about what direction he now wished
to head. The answer was out there, yet it frustratingly
remained just beyond his reach, whispering that if he
just stretched a little bit farther, the solution would come
to him. At some point he'd have to make a decision, but
thanks to careful financial planning, that point wasn't
right now. And with six months left on the lease on his
Manhattan apartment, he didn't need to worry about
moving just yet. Which was good as he had no idea
where he planned to live—other than to know it would
no longer be in fast-paced Manhattan.

So, in the meanwhile, he'd do what the doctor ordered. Rest. Relax. Toss off his all-work, no-play per-
sona and embrace the carefree, bachelor lifestyle. Hook
up with a bevy of gorgeous women. Not that he'd lived
like a monk before—but he'd certainly devoted a hell
of a lot more time to his job than to his social life. A
few years down the road, after he'd seen the world,
made up for lost dating time and had a new career going,
then he'd start looking around for Ms. Right.

You found her once, his inner voice chimed in slyly.
You had her. But you let her get away….

The mental picture he'd only moments ago success-
fully blocked now broke through his carefully erected
barriers and a vivid image of Mallory Altman rose in

his mind, filling him with the same sense of loss and regret the thought of her always brought.

Had ten years really passed since they'd first met? Nine years since that unforgettable summer when their friendship had caught fire and flared into a steaming love affair? Yes, although when he allowed himself to think about that summer, the memories remained so clear, so vivid, it didn't seem possible it had happened so long ago.

To this day, if he closed his eyes, he could still hear her infectious laugh. See her teasing grin. He'd loved her sense of humor, the magical way she could turn even the dullest chore into something fun. He'd fallen hard... so hard that the depth of his feelings had scared the crap out of him. Yeah, he'd had her, but the timing had been wrong. For both of them.

They'd been too young, his emotions too intense. She'd just turned eighteen and was headed off to a university hundreds of miles away, while he was only twenty-one, a new college grad about to start his Wall Street career. When he'd found himself thinking about forever— about marriage, kids and a mortgage, panic swamped him and he suggested they take a break. See other people. She'd agreed and he'd breathed a huge sigh of relief.

It hadn't taken him long to realize he'd made a mistake, but it had been long enough for her to find someone else. And to make it clear that Adam was now "just a friend." Losing her, realizing that her feelings hadn't run anywhere near as deep as his had hurt like a jagged blade through his heart.

They'd briefly run into each other a few times after

that, but each time they'd been involved with other people. He hadn't seen her in five years. Still, the image of her gorgeous smile and warm, chocolaty brown eyes remained as vibrant as ever. The last he'd heard about her had been three years ago when he'd seen an announcement in the paper that she'd gotten engaged.

An odd, unsettling numbness had invaded his chest at the news, and all the memories he'd so firmly locked away had ambushed him. The first time he'd seen her. First time he'd touched her. Kissed her. Made love to her. The last time he'd touched her…and all those touches in between. He'd tortured himself, letting down his guard to recall those incredible few weeks that had been the happiest of his life. Then he'd mentally wished her well and forced her from his mind—a feat he managed fairly well most of the time.

Now, he roughly shoved aside her image. Mallory was the past. His future was spread before him like a bachelor banquet filled with desirable women, no-strings sex, the European trip he'd always dreamed of, more desirable women and even more no-strings sex. He'd worked hard and now it was time to decompress and reap some benefits.

A bell tinkled, indicating that someone had entered the storefront, yanking him from his reverie. Must be the one o'clock appointment. As Nick had dashed out this morning after Annie's call announcing she was in labor, he'd asked Adam to reschedule the day's appointments. He'd been able to contact everyone except the one o'clock and two o'clock slots. Hopefully they'd both be understanding about the lack of photographer.

He didn't want to lose any customers for Nick in his absence.

Exiting the studio, he made his way down the short hallway toward the front of the store. When he entered the main room, he saw a dark-haired woman wearing a sleeveless turquoise dress standing in front of the glass-top counter, her back to Adam.

"Hi," he said, striding forward with a smile.

She turned and whatever else he'd planned to say drained from his head as his footsteps faltered, then stopped. And damn, it felt as if his heart did the same. Her brown eyes widened and she looked nearly as stunned as he felt. He wouldn't have believed she could look better than what his memory conjured up, but she did. More beautiful. More desirable. More tempting. And real.

How ironic, since timing had played such a pivotal role in their relationship and its demise, that she should walk through the door just when he'd been thinking about her.

Walking toward her, he cleared his throat to find his voice and spoke words he'd never thought he'd have the opportunity to say again.

"Hi, Mallory."

"Bring your knee up a little higher. Ooooh, yeah. Right there. Mallory...that's perfect."

Mallory Altman shifted on the smooth ivory satin sheets, the material cool and slick against her over-heated body. She felt like an overripe peach about to burst from its too-tight skin. Certainly not the way she'd anticipated feeling this afternoon. But then, she hadn't anticipated finding herself in Adam Clayton's company.

Even after not seeing him for five years, the sound of his deep, husky voice still shivered tingles down her spine. Good thing she was lying down because her knees felt positively mushy. Yet she'd felt mushy since the moment she'd so unexpectedly set eyes on him. She couldn't deny that over the past five years she'd found herself wondering if or when she might see him again. But never, not even in her wildest fantasies, had it ever occurred to her that it would happen like *this*.

She'd been so stunned to see him she'd barely managed to ask him what he was doing here, of all places. Left his job on Wall Street, he'd replied, much to her amazement, and was pitching in at Picture This to help out his best friend, Nick, whose wife had gone into labor that morning. There'd been little time for more conversation—she had a client to see in an hour, and he had another appointment. Once she'd changed into her lingerie for her boudoir-pictures photo shoot, everything had just moved so quickly, and talking had been the last thing on her mind.

Still, surely it was only this provocative situation that had her in this aroused state—and nothing to do with Adam himself. After all, what they'd shared together was long over. Besides, what woman wouldn't find herself aroused by lying on satin sheets, wearing exquisitely expensive silk lingerie while being photographed by a sexy, gorgeous man?

He'd always been attractive—not handsome in a pretty-boy, conventional way—but in a ruggedly masculine way that made it seem as if he spent all his time outdoors rather than on the floor of the New York Stock Exchange. With his thick dark hair and deep blue eyes, she'd liked the look of him the instant she'd laid eyes on him ten years ago.

An image flashed in her mind of the first time she'd seen him. She'd been seventeen and sulky, convinced her life was over because she and her mom had just relocated—for the sixth time in twelve years—from Chicago to Long Island, New York, forcing her to attend her upcoming senior year of high school at a new school. She'd prayed that her mother's position with the orchestra in Chicago would last just one more year, but no such luck.

As a professional cellist and financially strapped single mother, Emily Altman moved to whichever city's orchestra made her the best offer. Because of their transient lifestyle and the fact that money was forever tight, they'd always lived in apartments—until the move to Long Island where, as a concession to Mallory for leaving her friends and steady boyfriend, her mom had splurged and rented a small house. For Mallory, the profound sense of stability, of permanence, she'd felt at finally living in a house had almost made up for having to move again. She'd actually considered staying in Chicago, living with a girlfriend's family to finish out her last year of high school, but in the end she just couldn't let her mom go alone. Since Mallory's father had walked away before she'd been born rather than accept the responsibility of a pregnant girlfriend, Mallory and her mom had always been the two musketeers. So she'd packed up and moved. Again. And had met Adam.

He'd been twenty and friendly, home for the summer after completing his junior year of college. He'd been mowing the lawn at her house. At the ungodly hour of 8:30 a.m. on a Saturday. She'd been tempted to hurl a shoe out her bedroom window at him, but then he'd looked up and smiled at her and *whammo*—suddenly New York wasn't looking so bad. A friendship and easy camaraderie had been born. He'd made her laugh, and had amazed her when he said he'd lived in the same house his entire life. A year later, their friendship caught fire and for a beautiful, brief time, had burned out of control. A decade after that first meeting, his smile still had the power to affect her.

"Think about what you want to do to your lover," Adam said softly, jerking her attention back to the present. He looked at her through the lens of his Nikon and adjusted the focus. "Think about what you want your lover to do to you."

A memory, sharp and poignant, instantly materialized in Mallory's mind…of that incredible summer…of the first time they'd made love. Adam, scooping her up in his strong arms, his blue eyes hot with want as he carried her to his bed. She'd wanted so badly to touch him, taste him. And wanted him to do the same to her.

She'd been a virgin and nervous, expecting awkwardness, but they'd laughed over their brief fumbles, and then…pure magic. His hands…God, she remembered his hands so well…large and calloused, skimming down her body, touching her everywhere, followed by his lips, which had proved as magical as his hands. Her hands and mouth exploring him. Hot skin, murmured words, tangled sheets. And the way he'd looked at her, with such desire, reverence and need as he'd slowly entered her.

She was vaguely aware of the shutter snapping, but all her focus, all her concentration, was on the memories washing over her. And the fantasy of experiencing that heat with him again.

And that was really…

Bad. Wrong.

And damned inconvenient.

She closed her eyes and tried to visualize Greg—the man she *should* be thinking about. Greg. Her boyfriend. The man for whom she was having these provocative boudoir pictures taken. Her plan had been to reignite their stalled love life with a gift of these photos. Yet ever since she'd walked into the studio and discovered to her shock and consternation that Adam would be taking the pictures, her fine plan had disintegrated like steam in a wind storm. And speaking of steam…she felt as if it were pulsing from her every pore.

"Roll onto your side," Adam said, "and let the strap of your teddy fall off your shoulder…that's it. Now shake your head and wet your lips…perfect. You're beautiful, Mallory. Stunning. And sexy as hell."

You're beautiful, Mallory. Another memory slammed into her. A hot summer night. Adam's parents away for the weekend. Skinny-dipping in Adam's pool. Her legs wrapped tightly around his waist, his erection buried so deep in her body she didn't know where she ended and he began. His fingers slowly tracing her features as if trying to memorize them. His husky words whispering over her wet skin... *You're beautiful, Mallory.*

Blinking away the image, she managed to say, "I bet you say that to all the women you photograph."

He looked at her over the camera and she felt the impact of his regard all the way down to her feet. "No, I don't."

Heat seeped through her, and suddenly she *felt* beautiful. Stunning. Sexy. In that way he'd somehow always made her feel. A way she hadn't felt for a long time. If she *had* felt that way, she most likely wouldn't be here, trying this last-ditch effort to resuscitate her and Greg's sex life. But Adam's praise echoed in her ears, encouraging her to push aside her inhibitions.

Staring into the camera, into the place where she knew his dark blue eyes looked at her through the lens, she slowly rolled to her side, then rose to her knees, reveling in the cool slide of the black silk teddy against her heated skin, the delicious friction of the sheer stockings and lacy garter belt against her legs.

Do you remember, Adam? The question whispered through her mind. *Are you recalling, as I am, the way it was between us? How we couldn't keep our hands off each other? How you used to love to touch my hair like this...?*

Lifting her hands, she sifted her fingers through her loose hair, envisioning Adam...er, Greg—no, damn it, it was Adam—approaching her, lowering his head to kiss her. Her eyes drifted closed and her lips parted, anticipating the brush of his lips, the delicious sweep of his tongue, and again memories swept through her, of the first time he'd kissed her.

She'd gone to his house, intending to casually mention she'd broken up with her boyfriend, hoping Adam might ask her out. He'd answered the door dressed in jeans and a white T-shirt, his hair shower-damp, his skin smelling clean and fresh. He'd looked so delicious she'd nearly forgotten how to speak. Heart pounding, she'd told him her news. No sooner had the words passed her lips than he'd cupped her face between his hands, whispered *Thank God,* and then kissed her. A long, slow, deep, knee-weakening kiss that left no doubt he'd been experiencing the same pull of attraction as she. When he'd finally ended the kiss, he'd looked as dazed as she'd felt.

"Do you have any idea how long I've wanted to do that?" he'd asked.

"How long?"

"I met you a year ago, so…a year."

His confession had thrilled her and made her wish she'd broken up with her boyfriend a lot sooner. She'd smiled and pulled his head toward hers. "Seems we have a lot of time to make up for," she'd whispered against his lips.

"That's the end of the last roll."

At the sound of Adam's deep voice, Mallory's eyes popped open, dispelling the memory. He stepped from behind the camera and regarded her with an indecipherable expression.

The spell broken, heat crept up Mallory's neck, although why she should be embarrassed puzzled her. She hadn't done anything wrong. In fact, she was trying to do something *right*. For Greg. Reliving memories, fantasizing, was perfectly normal. Still, she sent up a mental prayer of thanks that Adam couldn't read minds. Or Greg, for that matter.

Yet she couldn't help but wonder if Adam's mind had been filled with similar sensual images while he'd snapped the photos. Probably not. The sexual fire that had burned between them had been short-lived and died out long ago. And while he held a special place in her heart since he'd been her first, the devastating ease with which he'd ended their relationship left no doubt she'd amounted to little more than a notch on his bedpost.

And now, here he was. Looking even more incredible than when she'd last seen him. And here she was. Wearing the three hundred dollars worth of La Perla lingerie she'd purchased to entice another man. A man named…um, Greg. Right. Greg.

With a self-conscious cough, she looked around for her robe. Perhaps Adam could read minds—not a comforting thought—because he plucked the pink terry-cloth garment from the chair next to his camera then walked toward her.

"Here you go," he said, handing her the robe, his eyes alight with the hint of mischief she so vividly recalled, "although it's a shame to cover up that lingerie."

Whew! Who the heck had turned on the heat? Didn't this room have air-conditioning? It was *July* for cryin' out loud. Even though she already felt as if she were melting, she quickly slipped on the thick robe, wrapping the material around herself and belting the sash.

Ah, that was better. Feeling much more in control

now that she was covered from neck to shin and it was no longer noticeable that her nipples were erect, she slid from the mattress and stood before him. Even though a respectable six feet separated them, she had to brace her knees to keep from backing up to put more distance between them.

There were dozens of questions she wanted to ask him—about his life, what he'd been doing for the past five years—but a quick glance at the wall clock indicated she had no time to socialize before meeting her client. In fact, she'd have to move if she didn't want to be late.

"When will the pictures be ready?" she asked, proud that she didn't sound as breathless as she felt.

"The proofs should be done within a week. I'll call you when they're finished." He rested his hands on his Levi's-clad hips, and Mallory pretended her peripheral vision wasn't working. Pretended she didn't notice how his splayed fingers seemed to point toward his groin. Pretended it wasn't obvious how great he looked in those jeans, which, based on the fascinating fade patterns, were old favorites. Of course, she'd also seen him wearing a suit and tie and he'd looked mighty fine in that, too. She suppressed a feminine sigh of pure appreciation. He was just that sort of guy—looked great no matter what he wore. Actually, as she well knew, he looked great wearing nothing at all.

"Earth to Mallory…you okay?"

She blinked. "Uh, yeah. Fine." She took two jerky steps back, toward the dressing room where she'd left her clothes. "I'd better get dressed." With that she turned and walked swiftly across the room.

After emerging five minutes later, feeling much more in control now that she was fully clothed, her sexy lingerie folded in her shopping bag, she made her way to the front of the studio. Adam stood behind the counter, writing on a pad next to the phone. When her heels clicked on the ceramic-tile floor, he looked up. Their gazes met and Mallory's footsteps nearly faltered.

Whoa. He packed a powerful wallop with a mere look. But then, he always had. Probably because of those gorgeous blue eyes that could change from teasing to intense in a heartbeat. The way he used to look at her, as if he could see into her soul…she gave herself a mental shake. It was better she not think about it. Adam was her past—and that's where he needed to stay.

He stepped from behind the counter. They met in the middle of the floor and he walked with her to the door. "It was great seeing you again, Mallory." He shot her a wicked, teasing smile and waggled his brows. "Especially seeing so much of you."

Heat rushed into Mallory's face. She nearly said that if she'd had the slightest inkling that he would have been taking her pictures, she would have chosen a different photography studio, but the words died in her throat. Not only did they sound unintentionally insulting, but she had the uncomfortable feeling that they might not be true.

"It was great seeing you, too, Adam." She imitated his brow waggle. "Even if you saw more of me than I saw of you."

Mischief, along with an unmistakable flash of interest, glittered in his eyes. "Perhaps on this particular occasion. Still, it's a problem that could have been solved like *that*." He snapped his fingers.

This time heat whooshed downward, warming Mallory all the way to her toes. "Not a good idea when one is taking pictures, I imagine," she said, matching his teasing tone. "I think that's called double exposure."

He laughed. "I'm sorry we didn't have much of a chance to catch up."

"Me, too. I would have loved to hear all about this big career change you've made."

"And I'd have loved to hear how your real-estate business is going and about this guy you had these pictures done for. He's a lucky man."

"Thank you."

"Maybe when you pick up your proofs you'd like to grab a cup of coffee together?"

A perfectly casual invitation that absolutely should not have revved her heartbeat the way it did. He was an old friend, for goodness sake. Nothing more. They'd had coffee together dozens of times. Obviously spending an hour in the afternoon wearing sexy lingerie had had a strange effect on her libido. To refuse would make it seem as if she placed too much importance on an offhand invite. "That sounds nice, Adam."

"Great. I'll call you when the proofs are ready." He smiled and opened the door for her.

"Talk to you soon," she said, then stepped out onto the sidewalk. She actually welcomed the blast of inferno-like July heat that engulfed her because it gave her something on which to blame her discomfort. Walking quickly to her car, she slid behind the wheel. She'd driven three blocks before her breathing returned to normal—a fact she refused to examine too closely for fear of discovering the reason.

Her life was finally exactly the way she wanted it. Stable. Secure. No more moving around the country, no more living in apartments. Her career was in high gear, and she'd recently achieved a milestone goal and bought her first house. She had a steady boyfriend who had a steady job—yup, everything was perfect and…steady.

Okay, maybe things weren't perfect with Greg, but she'd kissed enough frogs to know that he had prince potential. He provided the stability she'd always craved, and she was willing to work on the things that needed some polishing—like their sex life. Hey, not every guy could be like Adam Clayton in bed. Actually, she'd finally forced herself to admit that *no* guy would ever be like Adam Clayton in bed.

The last thing she wanted, or needed, was someone to rock the steady little boat she'd worked so hard for. She wouldn't allow that to happen. Nine years ago, Adam had capsized her. She wasn't about to give him the chance to do it again.

2

WITH THE SUNSHINE SENDING shimmering shafts of gold through the front window of Picture This, Adam stared at the contact sheets from his photo session with Mallory Altman and blew out a long, slow breath.

She looked…incredible. Soft and feminine. Wicked, yet somehow innocent. Tempting and enticing and aroused and so damn sexy he found himself shifting uncomfortably to relieve the strangulation occurring behind the fly of his jeans.

He supposed he shouldn't be surprised by his reaction. Hey, show him a guy who wouldn't be turned on by these pictures, and he'd show you a dead guy. He'd told her that her boyfriend was a lucky man, but what he should have said was her boyfriend was the luckiest damn guy in New York. And for a brief, magical time nine years ago, Adam had been that lucky guy.

Damn, seeing her again had felt like a punch in the heart. Stunned amazement followed by that mind-boggling rush of pleasure. The appointment book had read *M. Allory*—or at least that's what he'd thought it said, as Nick's handwriting was atrocious. One look at her, at her smile, at those brown eyes that had always reminded him of warm, melting chocolate, and the years had slipped away, inundating him with a flood of memories…memories that had haunted him all week and that threatened to take over now.

Forcibly pushing them aside, his gaze riveted on one particular photo of her. She was lying on her side on the bed, her dark hair spread across her shoulders in a disheveled fall of loose, shiny curls. With her head propped up on one hand, her other arm rested along the sinuous indent of her waist and the curve of her hip. One stocking-clad knee was bent, her moist lips slightly parted and her eyes stared directly into the camera. She looked like a succulent silk-clad morsel waiting to be plucked from an hors d'oeuvres platter. Actually, *daring* someone to pluck her from that platter.

A memory crystallized in his mind, of Mallory, lying in a similar position on top of his sleeping bag in the tent they'd pitched the weekend they'd gone camping upstate. Three glorious, lazy days spent almost exclusively in that tent, exploring each other, touching, talking, learning—each caress, each new bit of knowledge about her making him fall deeper in love. He could see her as if it were yesterday, her hair a dark, glossy tumble of curls. Wearing nothing but a playful, wicked grin. *See anything you like?* she'd asked in a smoky voice. He certainly had—and had delighted in showing her each and every thing.

He blinked away the lingering thought and again studied the photo. Her pose highlighted every gorgeous feminine curve and her eyes seemed to say *I am everything you could ever want and I'll make all your fantasies come true.* Definitely words any man would love to hear. Words the man in her life had no doubt heard.

A surge of what felt suspiciously like jealousy washed through him and he shook his head. Damn, he was losing his mind. Jealous over some guy he'd never met. But maybe it wasn't jealousy—maybe it was more like envy. Yeah, that's all it was. Envy. What guy wouldn't want a woman to go to the effort of taking sexy pictures for him? To look at him like he was the only man on earth and she wanted to gobble him up in one bite? The fact that she'd taken such sexy photos proved she still possessed the adventurous sense of fun he'd found so captivating. Whoever Mallory's man was, he was one lucky bastard and Adam hoped the guy appreciated what he had. It was certainly something Adam wished *he* had.

That thought brought him up short and a frown yanked down his brows. What the hell was he thinking? He didn't want that. A woman didn't spend the time and money to have such intimate photos taken for a man unless they were in a *relationship.* Unless she had *strong feelings* for him. And relationships and strong feelings were the last things on Adam's current three-months-in-Europe, bachelor agenda. Mallory had wreaked havoc on his travel plans once before. She was the sort of woman he suspected could also wreak havoc with a guy's bachelor plans. Good thing she wasn't available.

His gaze drifted back down to the contact sheets. He'd lost touch with Mallory five years ago, right after his life had taken such a dramatic turn due to his dad's unexpected death. Hadn't seen her since.

Well, he'd seen her again now. And damn, he'd liked everything he'd seen. And everything he'd seen had dredged up those memories he'd tried so hard to bury. But unfortunately those memories had haunted him constantly this past week.

He'd been stunned to learn she wasn't married. During their brief chat last week, he'd made a comment about the photos being for her husband and she'd told him they were for her boyfriend—that her engagement had ended before the wedding had taken place.

Pulling his gaze away from the photos, he looked at his watch. Just past noon. Would she come into the studio today to pick up her proofs? He'd called her this morning—shaking his head as he recalled how his heart had pounded. An answering machine had clicked on after the third ring and a recorded voice had asked that he leave a message. After saying that her proofs were ready, he'd hung up, feeling ridiculously let down that he hadn't had a chance to talk to her.

His thoughts were interrupted when the front door opened. Adam's heart jumped only to settle back into place when Nick Daly walked into the studio. Friends since high school, Nick was the brother Adam had never had—yet in all those years, he'd never seen Nick look more bleary-eyed or rumpled.

"How is it possible for a guy to look so exhausted and so happy at the same time?" Adam asked with a grin.

"If you expect me to answer any complicated questions, you've lost your mind."

He took in the colossal foam coffee cup clutched in Nick's hand. "I didn't know the Java Hut made to-go cups that big."

"Trust me, there isn't a container big enough for the caffeine hit I need," Nick said with a tired smile. "I think I should just request an IV drip. Sorry to be so late."

"No problem. That's why I'm here—to hold down the fort for the proud new dad."

A grin that could only be described as totally besotted curved Nick's mouth. "Oh, man, Adam, I don't think there's ever been a more beautiful baby in the history of babies than Caroline."

"Can't argue with you there. I was the proudest honorary uncle at the nursery when I visited her at the hospital. But I bet your parents said the same thing about you when you were born." He made a great show of looking Nick over. "Then again, maybe they didn't."

"Ha-ha. Tread carefully, my friend. You're dealing with someone who's had about seven hours of sleep in the last seven days. Caroline may be adorable and gorgeous, but whew, can that kid *yell*. Gotta tell ya, whoever made up that phrase 'sleep like a baby' clearly never spent any time with an actual baby because let me tell you—babies do not sleep. At least not for more than like twenty minutes at a time. And you know what? When the baby isn't asleep, the parents aren't asleep." He stifled a yawn. "Things will be easier after Annie's mom arrives the day after tomorrow to help out. Nothing like having a doting grandma on the premises. Annie and I'll finally get some sleep and I can get back to work. And you'll be off the hook."

Adam dragged a hand through his hair. "Listen, I still feel bad about leaving—"

Nick held up his hand to cut off the words. "Do not feel bad. You've wanted to take this trip as long as I've known you. Hell, you even scheduled it so you'd be around for a few weeks after the baby was born. Who knew she'd decide to be two weeks late?" He shook his head and grinned. "Typical female. But don't worry— uber-grandma is coming to the rescue."

"How's Annie doing?" Adam asked, wondering if she was as frazzled as her husband.

"Terrific. Same as me—thrilled, exhausted, totally in love with our daughter. Looking forward to her mom's two-week visit." He lifted the cup to his lips and took a long, deep swallow. "Maybe if I drink five more of these I'll be able to stay awake till lunchtime."

"It's lunchtime *now*."

Nick looked at his watch then shook his head. "Damn. How are today's bookings? Saturday's my busiest day."

"Relax. Everything's fine. I told you—I juggled things around so Kevin's handling the Baxter wedding. He's also doing the Anderson anniversary party for you tomorrow."

"Yeah, I know you told me. My brain's just not firing on all cylinders. Thanks for stepping in. I really appreciate it."

"No problem. I may not be an experienced photographer, but organization is right up my alley."

"You've known enough to keep me afloat till things calm down at home."

"Yeah, and I work cheap, too."

"Good. 'Cause with the extra money I'm going to have to pay Kevin, I can't afford to pay you much. Do you know how much baby stuff costs? *Major* bucks, my friend. Which, by the way, Annie and I want to thank you for all the stuff you've bought Caroline. The clothes, books, dolls. They're great. I never knew you liked to shop."

"I never had the time—or an adorable princess to buy for. I can't wait till she's old enough for video games."

Nick laughed. "I bet." He approached the counter and nodded his chin at the proof sheets. "What're those?"

"Contact sheets from some photos I took last week." At Nick's surprised look, Adam said, "I guess I should have told you, but it seemed like you had enough on your plate. Last week when Annie went into labor and you dashed out of here like your shorts were on fire, you told me to reschedule the day's studio appointments—"

"I remember."

"Well, I was able to reach everyone except two. So when the customers arrived, I took the pictures."

Nick's brows raised. "How'd you do?"

Adam slid the glossy proof sheets across the counter. "You tell me."

Nick glanced at the proofs, then did a double take. "Ah, the boudoir pics that were scheduled. I was supposed to take them."

"Can't say I was real disappointed I had to pinch-hit for you, buddy."

"Jccz, I guess not," Nick said, sliding the proof sheets nearer.

"It was my intention to ask her to reschedule when she arrived, but I took one look at her and 'wanna reschedule' came out as 'Adam Clayton, photographer, at your service.'"

"Can't say I blame you." Leaning closer, Nick carefully examined the photos. "I gotta say, these are really good."

"Thanks. But look what I had to work with."

"She's beautiful," Nick agreed. "Still, for a guy who spent all his time at the stock exchange, you've got a great eye for a photograph."

"Even though it's been a while, I still remember my way around a camera lens from high school."

Nick grinned. "Yeah—how geeky were we? The president and vice president of the photography club."

"Hey, it was a great way to meet girls."

"Sure was." Nick straightened. "Look, I know you're looking to make a career change—you might want to consider coming on board. I want to expand the business, and if this is the type of work you can do without really even knowing what the hell you're doing…well, I'm impressed."

"Well, you might not be so impressed when you see the proofs of the other shots I took that day. After how great the first session went, I admit I was feeling pretty confident. So when Mrs. Wentworth showed up with her twins, I figured I'd take those pictures, as well."

"And?"

Adam slid another manila envelope toward Nick. "Read 'em and weep."

Nick slid the sheets from the envelope and winced when he saw the first one.

"I had a hell of a time," Adam said, raking his hands through his hair. "Nothing was cooperating. Not the equipment, not Mrs. Wentworth, and least of all the twins. You think one baby makes a lot of noise? Try two. It's deafening. Not to mention nerve-racking."

"Welcome to my world." Nick pointed to one print showing a pair of red-faced, teary-eyed, screaming one-year-olds. "They do not look happy."

Adam glanced at the shot. "Yeah? Well, that's the happiest they were the whole time. Listen, I'm looking for a low-pressure, non-stress job and with the Wentworth gig, I could practically feel my blood pressure rising."

Nick shook his head. "These are awful, dude."

"I agree. Clearly I'm only good at taking pictures of sexy women wearing lingerie."

Nick grinned. "Well, if you've got to be good at something…"

Adam laughed. "Right." He paused, then said, "Actually, she wasn't just any woman. I know her. She used to live not five miles from here, and only a few blocks from my family."

"Hell, I lived only a few blocks from your family." He looked at the picture again. "Face isn't ringing any bells. What's her name?"

"Mallory Altman."

Nick shook his head. "Not familiar, but you always had more girls than I could keep track of."

"You and I had already graduated from high school when Mallory and her mom moved here from Chicago. I used to mow her lawn during the summer."

"Man, you scored more chicks with that landscaping job. Helluva lot more than I did working in the photo lab."

"Yeah, but that's where you eventually found Annie and ended up with the real prize."

"That I did." He nodded toward the photos of Mallory. "So, anything ever happen between you two?"

He hesitated. He'd never told Nick about his love affair with Mallory. Nick had spent that summer traveling as part of a photography course. By the time he'd returned, Adam's relationship with Mallory was over and he hadn't wanted to talk about it. Even now he still felt reluctant to tell Nick about his past intimate relationship with Mallory. "We were good friends."

Clearly Nick deduced everything he needed to know in Adam's hesitation because he nodded knowingly. "Gotcha. So why'd you break up? Was she lousy in bed?"

God. No. She'd been...perfect. "The timing just wasn't right."

"How's the timing now?"

"She had these taken for her boyfriend."

"Bummer, dude."

"Nah. She's the past. I'm looking forward to the future. Besides, I'd categorize her as a 'long-term' sort of woman—and right now, my 'long-term' is three, maybe four hours."

Nick turned toward the front picture window and cleared his throat. "Speak of the devil…here comes your lingerie-wearing friend now."

Adam looked toward the glass door and his heart performed a crazy somersault at the sight of Mallory striding across the street. Dressed in a bright pink sleeveless top and a full ivory skirt dotted with splashes of matching pink that flirted just above her knees, and cream high heels, she looked lovely, cool, feminine, and…really, really tempting. Like an ice-cream cone on a hot day from which you wanted to take a nice long lick.

He'd just finished sliding her proofs back into the envelope when she entered the studio.

"Hi, Adam," she said with a smile. "I got your message about the proofs."

"Hi, Mallory." After uttering those two words, his powers of speech seemed to go into a holding pattern and he found himself staring at her, uncharacteristically tongue-tied. She'd pulled back her dark glossy hair into a loose, attractive knot, which left her neck bare. Her big brown eyes were surrounded by thick dark lashes, and the same smattering of gilt freckles he recalled paraded across her nose.

Unfortunately thoughts of freckles had him picturing the trio of dots he knew formed a triangle beneath her left breast. And the single tiny spot that graced the curve of her right buttock. Gorgeous, enticing spots he'd explored with his fingers and lips, tasted with his tongue.

Shoving the distracting images aside, he concentrated on her mouth. *Oh, yeah, like that's less distract-*

ing, his inner voice snickered. Her lips were just as he recalled, too—full and moist and currently highlighted with some sort of luscious-looking pink gloss. He knew exactly how those delectable lips felt and tasted: soft, plump, smooth and delicious. Knew exactly how her tongue felt rubbing against his—

Nick's loud, pointed throat clearing jerked him from his reverie. After he'd introduced her to Nick, Mallory said to him, "Congratulations on your new baby."

"Thanks. Hey, want to see her picture?"

"Love to." She grinned. "As a photographer, I bet you just happen to have one or two."

"More like one or two thousand," Adam said with a laugh as Nick reached for his wallet.

"Oh, she's adorable," Mallory said, looking at the image of Caroline.

"Nick's going to be sweeping guys off the front porch," Adam teased.

Nick shot him "the look." "Since she can't date until she's thirty, I have some time to purchase my broom."

"Spoken like a true father of a daughter," Mallory said, chuckling. "I think all dads swear the same thing."

"And how does it work out?" Nick asked.

"You probably don't want to know."

They all laughed, then Adam handed her the manila envelope containing her proofs. "Here you go."

"Thanks. How'd they turn out?"

Incredible. Too incredible. I haven't been able to erase them—or you—from my mind. "I think they're great, if I may say so myself, but it's what you think that matters." He glanced at the clock. "Do you have time for that cup of coffee? Or maybe even lunch?"

She hesitated for several seconds then nodded. "I have about an hour before I have to meet my next client."

Adam refused to acknowledge the relief and anticipation that surged through him at her acceptance of his invitation. "Great." He turned to Nick. "Think you can stay awake for an hour?"

"Yeah. Maybe. Probably. Hell, I don't know. As long as I don't sit down or close my eyes there's a chance." He lifted his colossal cup and waggled it. "Bring me another of these and a sandwich, okay?"

"You bet."

Nick smiled. "I'll be in the darkroom. I happen to have a few more rolls of film of Caroline to develop."

"Only a few?" Adam teased. He looked at Mallory and shook his head. "That child is only a week old and already she's had more photographs taken of her than the president."

"Wait till *you* have a kid," Nick said. "We'll see how many pictures you take." He yawned. "And how much sleep you get."

With a wave, Nick headed toward the darkroom and Adam escorted Mallory across the room. Holding the door for her, her shoulder lightly brushed against his chest as she crossed the threshold and he sucked in a sharp breath at the contact. Then he inwardly frowned. How the hell could such a nothing touch affect him so strongly?

Because it's Mallory, his inner voice informed him,

and he realized it was true. It had always been that way with her and clearly some things never changed.

He caught an elusive whiff of a deliciously feminine, floral fragrance, which sizzled a bolt of heat through him that had nothing to do with the ninety-degree weather.

He gritted his teeth. Damn, if a mere brush and a whiff affected him like this, what the hell would happen if she really touched him? If he really touched her?

Based on their past relationship, there wasn't a doubt in his mind. Fireworks. Spontaneous combustion.

But thanks to his traveling bachelor plans and her relationship, that wasn't in the cards. Which was for the best since Mallory didn't even come close to fitting into his traveling-the-world, woman-in-every-port bachelor plans.

Still, in spite of his best efforts not to think them, he couldn't stop the words that echoed through his mind:

Talk about lousy timing….

3

THE INSTANT MALLORY EXITED Picture This, a blast of hot air engulfed her and she suppressed a grimace. Thanks to her accidental brushing against Adam's chest, she needed more heat like she needed a hole in her head. But at least she could blame the un-wanted all-over body flush she'd experienced on the weather.

"Nothing like a heat wave in New York in July," she remarked, her tone miraculously casual considering how…un-casual she felt. "It's supposed to hit one hun-dred today. And tomorrow."

Adam groaned. "Tell me again why we're working and not at the beach?"

Instantly images of them together at the beach flipped through her mind like a tormenting slide show. Hot bodies submerged in cool ocean water. Touching, rubbing, caressing, his hands sliding beneath her swim-suit, her fingers exploring through his.

Had he purposely mentioned the beach to trigger memories? She glanced at him, but his expression was innocence itself. Too innocent? Maybe. Well, if he wanted to play "Let's Reminisce," she was game.

"The reason we're not at the beach is because clearly we're insane." She pointed to the building on the next corner. "How about the diner?"

Their gazes locked, then a slow smile curved his lips. Her heart seemed to lurch sideways. Was he thinking about the one time they'd gone to that diner? He satisfied her curiosity by saying, "The Stardust Diner. For old times' sake. Sounds great."

Less than five minutes later they were seated in a booth near the rear of the bustling diner, ensconced in blissful air-conditioning with frosty glasses of ice water and leather-bound menus set in front in them. Mallory took a much-needed sip of her drink, noting with annoyance that her hand gripping the glass wasn't quite steady.

Ridiculous. It was simply ridiculous that she felt this…unraveled in his presence. But there was no denying she did, and that annoyed her. As did the Greg-induced guilt that kept nudging her. *It's just lunch,* she told her overactive conscience. She'd enjoy the meal with an old friend, reminisce, catch up, and that would be the end of it. Nothing wrong with that.

Feeling better after her quick mental pep talk, she didn't open her menu, just pushed it to the end of the table.

"Already know what you want?" he asked with a smile.

You. Naked and sweaty. The inappropriate thought popped into Mallory's mind with the sudden shock of a cobra strike and she barely contained the horrified *Ack!* that rose to her lips.

Oh, boy, this was *not* good. She should *not* have accepted this invitation. And for a few seconds after he'd issued it, she'd considered saying no. But her idiotic pride had shot her better judgment aside with a well-placed arrow. *If you refuse, any excuse you give will sound like just that—an excuse. Then he'll wonder why you really didn't want to have a simple, innocent lunch with him.* Yes—and she certainly didn't want him to think that the real reason was that she'd been thinking about him all week—in ways she shouldn't have been thinking about him. Remembering him naked and sweaty. Wondering if his skin still felt the same. Tasted the same.

"You okay, Mallory?"

His concerned voice yanked her back to reality. "I'm fine. Just a little...overheated." And she sent up a mental prayer of thanks that it was July and not January or else he'd think she was nuts.

"So what are you going to order?"

If only he'd phrased his question like that the first time, maybe she wouldn't be in this painfully-aware-of-him situation. She heaved a mental sigh. No, she'd still be in this same situation. "I'm getting the usual."

"A bacon cheeseburger, side of onion rings and a chocolate shake?"

A wave of unwanted pleasure washed over her. "We came here *once.* You remember what I ordered?"

"Yup. I was impressed. Every other girl I knew would have ordered a salad with the dressing on the side. Especially if she was wearing a prom dress."

Their gazes met and there was no holding back the flood of memories that swamped her. Sitting in this very diner at 5:00 a.m. the night—or rather morning—after her senior prom. She was dressed in her pale green formal, Adam was in his dad's black tux. Her boyfriend from Chicago had gotten sick and couldn't travel to New York to escort her. Adam, already home from college for the summer, had gallantly offered to step in. It was the night that had marked the beginning of the change in their relationship. The night she'd realized she could no longer ignore the powerful attraction she felt for him.

"You were my knight in shining armor," she said, unable to control the slight hitch in her voice.

He laughed. "More like your knight in an ill-fitting tux."

"Are you kidding? You were gorgeous. I was the envy of every girl there. Especially since you were a college man."

"The way I recall it, you were the gorgeous one and I was the envy of every guy there."

More pleasure washed through her at his words and she inwardly scowled at herself for being such a sucker for flattery. "Hardly. But still, I'll never forget how sweet you were, picking me up in your Jeep—"

"The limo of champions—"

"—which you'd washed and waxed for the occasion. And the orchid corsage. Do you know, I still have that flower? It's pressed between the pages of my yearbook. I must have looked at that flattened orchid a thousand times that summer after the prom."

That summer after the prom...

The words hung between them and she could tell by the way his eyes darkened that he recalled how they'd spent those few magical weeks.

"How come you looked at the corsage?"

She hesitated, then decided what the hell, there was no harm in telling him after all these years. "It reminded me of you."

"A flattened, brown, dried-out flower. Gee, thanks a lot."

She laughed at his arid tone. "I meant it reminded me of that night. Of what a great time I had. Because of you."

He studied her for several seconds over the rim of his water glass, his steady gaze shooting tingles down her spine. "I had a great time, too."

Determined to prove to herself that their past was something she could discuss with breezy nonchalance, she gave a light laugh. "You were such a perfect gentleman that night...and I so badly didn't want you to be."

He lowered his glass to the table. "If it makes you feel any better, it practically killed me to be such a perfect gentleman," he said in an equally light tone. "You were so beautiful, and you smelled so good. All those slow dances? I thought I was going to lose my mind."

She recalled the delicious sensation of being held in his arms while they swayed to the music. His hard body brushing against hers. The forbidden thrill she'd experienced knowing she'd aroused him. The agony of wanting to kiss him, touch him, explore all the urgent, impossible-to-ignore feelings he inspired. Her honor preventing her from giving in. The guilt she'd felt about feeling so powerfully attracted to Adam when she already had a boyfriend. Sort of like the way she was feeling right—

She ruthlessly cut off *that* thought before it went any further.

"I guess you could say that was the night that changed things between us," Adam said softly.

She nodded. There was no denying that night had added fuel to the flame that had been flickering in her heart for months. Less than a week later, it flared into an inferno and they'd gone from friends to lovers.

"As far as I'm concerned," he continued, "the prom theme might as well have been *Gentlemen, start your engines.* I think I made my move about thirty seconds after you broke up with your boyfriend."

Yes. And it had been the longest thirty seconds she'd ever had to endure.

His gaze searched hers. "That was a great summer."

"Yes, it was." The most memorable of her life. Of course, it wasn't necessary that she share that tidbit of info with him.

A half smile pulled up his lips. "Remember the day we rented the boat?"

In a heartbeat a wealth of sensual memories crammed into her mind, obliterating everything else, and a breathy laugh escaped her. "Didn't catch many fish, did we?"

"Fish? That wasn't why we rented the boat."

Dear God, no, it wasn't. She barely resisted the urge to press her glass of ice water against her heated face.

He leaned forward, resting his elbows on the table, his gaze steady on hers. He was so close, less than an arm's length away. Much too close.

"It was to see how many times we could make love in a single afternoon," he said softly. "Your idea, as I recall."

Fire raced through her, recalling that glorious day spent in naked splendor in complete privacy in the quiet cove they'd found. Gentle waves slapping against the hull, hot sun, the scent of salt water and sunshine mixed with the musk of their passion.

She had to swallow to find her voice. "My idea," she agreed. "Although I didn't hear any complaints."

"Hell, no."

Oh, boy. Flames licked under her skin at the turn of this conversation, the barrage of sensual images of the past it inspired. She needed to steer the subject to safer waters. Immediately.

"And now look at us," she said, proud of her coolly amused tone, "almost ten years later, back at the old Stardust Diner. Eating the same artery-clogging food."

"All because you came into Picture This last week." He looked at her with an indecipherable expression. "I guess what they say about timing being everything is true."

"Yes." And it occurred to her that their entire past had been determined by the whims of timing. First she'd had a boyfriend. Then Adam had suggested they were too young to embark on an exclusive relationship. Then the few subsequent times they'd seen each other, they'd both been involved with someone.

Their timing now wasn't any better—not that it mattered, of course. They were way past their youthful affair. Still, she couldn't deny it gave her a feminine thrill to know he remembered so many details of their time together. Following immediately on the heels of that feminine thrill was an undeniable sense of curiosity mixed with loss. What might have happened if their timing hadn't always been so bad?

Their gazes locked and a tingle zoomed through her at the speculation in his eyes. Could he be thinking the same thing? Not that it mattered. Not a bit. Nope.

The waitress appeared at their table and she welcomed the interruption of her runaway thoughts. "Ready to order?"

Adam laid his menu, unopened, on top of hers. "Two bacon cheeseburgers, two orders of onion rings, two chocolate shakes."

After the waitress left, Mallory said, "Not a meal I indulge in often anymore, but on the rare occasion I come to this diner, it's a must-have. For old times' sake."

"Nothing wrong with indulging yourself. For old times' sake."

Again their gazes held and Mallory swore something flashed in his eyes. Something that curled more of that unwanted and unsettling heat through her veins. The last thing she wanted to think about while within fifty yards of Adam Clayton was indulging herself. Definitely time get this conversation back on course.

Leaning her elbows on the Formica table she said, "Okay, spill it. What have you been doing for the past five years?"

"I can pretty much sum it up in one word—*working*. You?"

"Oh, no. You don't get off that easily."

He leaned back and shrugged. "I'm not exaggerating. I'd just completed and passed all the reviews and qualifications necessary to purchase my own seat on the stock exchange when my father died."

He paused and Mallory easily read the sadness in his eyes. The last time she'd seen Adam before she'd walked into Picture This last week had been at his dad's funeral. Adam had looked pale and drawn, his expression bleak, and her heart had broken for him and his family. Without thinking, she reached out and laid her hand over his.

And instantly realized her error.

She'd meant it only to be a friendly gesture of sympathy, an innocent show of understanding, but there was nothing innocent about the jolt of desire that shot through her by touching him. Her first reaction was to snatch her hand away as if he'd burned her, but that would make her look like an idiot. And God help her, she really liked the way his warm, strong hand felt beneath hers.

After licking her suddenly dry lips, she whispered, "I'm so sorry, Adam. I know how close you and your father were."

He glanced down at her hand resting on his and a muscle jerked in his jaw. "He was only forty-eight."

"I know." She gently withdrew her hand, then settled it on her lap, so she could clasp her fingers together to retain the warmth of his skin without him knowing.

Looking up, he rested his gaze on hers. "There's no doubt that the stress of the job contributed greatly to his heart attack, and I could easily see the exact same thing happening to me a few years down the road. He willed his seat on the exchange to me, and my first reaction was to just sell it. Walk away. And I almost did. But I felt such a connection to him there. I found I couldn't just abandon all the plans we'd made together."

"So you stayed."

"Yes. Took over the seat. But I promised myself I wouldn't let what happened to him happen to me. I wasn't going to work myself into an early grave. I gave myself until my thirty-fifth birthday as a deadline—that was enough time to save and plan and also a good time to reassess my life and goals. So, for the last five years I worked like a dog. Devoted all my time and energy to the job. Saved and invested wisely. Good thing, because three months ago, fate stepped in in the form of chest pains."

Her shocked concern must have shown on her face because he quickly shook his head. "Not a heart attack. Doctor said it was stress. That if I didn't change my life-style, reduce my stress levels, learn to relax, given my family history I was headed in the exact direction I'd sworn I'd never take. Couple weeks later I sold my seat on the exchange. Called it a thirtieth birthday present to myself—a gift that would insure I was around to celebrate my fortieth and live to a ripe old age."

"So you've been working at Picture This for the past two months?"

"No. My mom and grandmother moved to South

Carolina after my dad died. I spent the first three weeks visiting them." A crooked smile curved his lips. "It was great. I hadn't taken a vacation in five years, and they spoiled me rotten. Home-cooked meals every night, sleeping in late. I can't remember the last time I felt so relaxed.

"Then I spent the next month finishing the basement in Nick's house for him. With the baby on the way, he needed the extra room, and I really enjoyed working with my hands again. Nothing like hammering in Sheet-rock and smearing Spackle to clear the mind."

A memory of him, shirtless, sweaty, gorgeous, wielding a hammer as he built a shed in his family's backyard, flashed through her mind, leaving a trail of heat in its wake. Forcing a smile, she said, "I'll take your word for it—but I recall that you liked to spackle and smear."

"Yup. When I finished the basement, Nick asked me if I'd like to pitch in at the studio until after the baby was born. Since I had the time and hadn't decided what I wanted to do career-wise yet, I figured why not? I started two days before you walked through the door."

Her brows shot upward. "Two days? Just how much experience do you have as a photographer?"

He grinned. "You were my first customer."

Fire rushed into her cheeks. She folded her arms across her chest and drummed her fingers against her arm, half annoyed, half amused. "You failed to mention that before I started posing in my lingerie."

"Damn right. Do you think I'm stupid?"

"Incorrigible is more like it."

"A minute ago I was a knight in shining armor."

"Times change."

He held up his hands in mock surrender. "Hey, it's not as if I'd never used a camera before. You're looking at the former vice president of Kennedy High School's photography club."

Her lips twitched. "A ringing endorsement."

He didn't add, *And it's not as if I haven't seen you wearing less,* but he didn't need to—the heated gleam in his eyes said it all. And made her want to squirm in her seat.

"Take a look at the pictures," he said. "If you don't like them, I'll reschedule you so Nick can take them."

The instant the words left Adam's mouth, he felt a frown pull down his brows. Somehow the thought of Nick taking photos of Mallory in her sexy lingerie didn't sit well.

Cripes, he was really losing his marbles. Nick was happily married. And Mallory had a boyfriend—the guy these pictures were taken for. And somehow that thought didn't sit well, either. Damn.

And it suddenly hit him that this lunch hadn't been a good idea. Seeing her, spending time with her, reminiscing with her, remembering how she'd felt in his arms, under him, over him, wrapped around him, was serving no purpose other than to torture him—something he hadn't really expected. So why the hell was he tortured? She was taken. Unavailable. He was about to head for Europe for three months as a carefree bachelor. Available for a fling with any woman who struck his fancy. He and Mallory were wrong for each other in every way.

Yet even knowing that, the mere sight of her seemed to turn him inside out. It wouldn't be so bad if he weren't still so damned attracted to her, but he was. Painfully so. But he couldn't just stand up and leave. He'd have to see this through. Besides, standing up wasn't a good idea if he didn't want to advertise exactly how her nearness affected him.

And damn it, how annoying was that? He was a grown man—not some horny, hormonal teenager who couldn't control his body. Yeah—a statement that had been perfectly true until he'd sat across from her. Looked into those warm brown eyes. Shared memories of the past. Of them naked, making love all afternoon on a rented boat. Until she'd touched him. Then in a heartbeat it was goodbye in-control-grown-man, hello hard-on. Definitely not good.

"I'm anxious to see the photos," she said, "but the waitress is approaching with our food. I'd better wait till after we eat so I don't get bacon cheeseburger on the pictures."

Forcefully redirecting his thoughts to their lunch, he said, "Good idea. Nothing worse than cholesterol on your lingerie." *Oh, that's brilliant—the perfect way to lose the hard-on. Think of her in that satin teddy.*

As soon as the waitress left, Adam raised his burger in a toast, determined to eat his lunch then get the hell out of Dodge. "Here's to old times."

"And old friends," she said with a smile, tapping the edge of her bun against his.

Adam took a bite, then groaned. If he had to suffer through a torturous lunch, at least it was with the best-tasting burger he'd ever eaten. He swallowed, then looked at Mallory, whose eyes were closed in ecstasy as she chewed, and he went perfectly still.

Damn. How did she manage to look so unbelievably sexy eating a freakin' hamburger? He didn't know, but he couldn't deny he'd always found it incredibly arousing that she enjoyed food with such abandon.

After she swallowed, Mallory opened her eyes and grinned. "Wow. I feel like I need a cigarette—and I don't even smoke. And that's after just one bite." She bit into an oversize onion ring and moaned. "Ooooh, baby. That is soooo good." She reached out her hand. "Taste."

Adam instantly recalled how she liked to share food. A crystal-clear memory of them, sharing a chocolate ice-cream cone, laughing, licking, sugary tongues dancing, chilled lips touching, slammed into his mind, skimming another layer of heat beneath his skin. After that ice cream, they'd parked on a dark, quiet street and made love in the backseat of his car.

With the memory fresh in his mind, and unable to stop himself, he leaned forward and took a bite of her offering. His lips inadvertently brushed against her fingertips, yet she appeared not to notice.

He wished like hell he hadn't noticed.

This damn meal was growing more torturous by the minute. And he feared that if it didn't end soon, she'd realize that he was all but enveloped in a cloud of lust.

While he chewed, he watched her pop the last bit into her mouth. "I'm going to want these bad boys every day," she said, casting a wistful glance at her plate of onion rings. Then she turned her attention to her shake and took a long draw.

"How is it?" Adam asked, his gaze riveted on the way her full glossy lips surrounded the red-and-white-striped straw. He had to swallow to stifle a groan. When the hell had watching a woman *drink* become so erotic?

"I can sum it up in one word—*ohmigod.*"

Adam tasted his shake and nodded in agreement, hoping the icy slide down his throat would help cool his overheated body.

"So what are your plans for your future?" she asked.

Thank God—something to concentrate on other than her lips. And red-hot memories of those lips wrapped around him instead of that straw.

"For my immediate future, travel. I'm leaving the day after tomorrow for my long-awaited trek around Europe."

"I remember you always wanted to go…" Her voice trailed off and he could clearly see she recalled he'd planned to go the summer after his college graduation. The summer she'd thrown all his plans into disarray. "You've never made it over there?"

"Nope. I'll be gone three months. After that, I'm planning a safari to Africa. Australia, South America and Asia are also on my to-do list. Somewhere in there I'll have to find a new place to live. My Manhattan lease is up in six months."

"Any ideas?"

"Not Manhattan. My doctor suggested a hut on a beach somewhere. He recommended Hawaii." He grinned. "Maybe I'll move there and open a tiki bar."

"Sounds…exciting. What about your future career plans?"

"From a financial standpoint I don't need to decide right away, so I'm still mulling them over." He took another icy pull of his shake then said, "And now that I've spilled all about me, what have you been doing for the past five years?"

"Same as you. Working. Building my client base."

"You enjoy working in real estate?"

"I do. I like every aspect of it—buyers, sellers, the challenge of matching up the right client with the right house. The housing market on Long Island has almost always been on the upswing, but it's really hopping right now. I've started dealing with some commercial properties, which is a great opportunity for me, and I'm preparing to earn my broker's license." After swallowing another bite of onion ring, she added, "Six months ago I bought my first house."

He could see how pleased she was and he raised his shake in a toast. "Congratulations. I know how much you always wanted your own house. That stability."

"Still do. I'm settled in, with a mortgage, a backyard, neighbors, block parties, the whole enchilada. It would take a nuclear blast to uproot me."

"Is your mother still moving around the country?"

"After stints in Miami and Dallas, she moved back here and is playing for the Long Island Philharmonic. She has an apartment in Suffolk County. Who knows how long she'll stay, but for now she's content."

"Glad to know your professional life is going so well." His glance involuntarily flicked to the manila envelope she'd propped against her seat, and a bolt of pure lust sizzled through him at the thought of those sexy pictures. "Seems like your personal life is, too."

Something flashed in her eyes. "Yup. Going great. How about you?"

His masculine pride wished he could say, *Yeah, women are lined up ten deep outside my apartment,* but he wasn't about to lie to her. Still, now that he had time, that situation was about to change. Especially with his trip to Europe. He was a mere plane ride away from gorgeous women lounging on exotic beaches. Ibiza, the French Riviera. Oooh, yeah.

"Everything's great. You know, doing the bachelor thing."

"Anyone special?"

"Nope."

"Hot date tonight?" she asked in a teasing voice.

"Nope."

"C'mon. I bet there're probably women lined up ten deep outside your door."

He swallowed his laugh at how precisely her words had echoed his thoughts. Right from day one of their friendship it had been almost eerie how they'd so often been on the same wavelength. "Not quite *ten* deep," he said with a smile. "My only date tonight is working at the studio to help Nick get caught up on paperwork."

"Bachelor-man doing paperwork on a Saturday night?" She made an exaggerated show of looking him over. "Unless your character has taken a total dive south, you're a fairly decent guy. Reasonably attractive. Heterosexual. Financially secure. Just the sort to attract a woman or two. So what's the problem?"

"No problem. Just taking a night off from the usual bachelor frivolity to help out a friend." *Right. No problem. Except I haven't been able to think of anyone except you for the past week.*

And it suddenly occurred to him that she'd been in his thoughts for a lot longer than the past week. She'd *always* been there, lingering in the back of his mind, and he'd compared every woman who'd come after her with the standard she'd set. As of yet, no one had surpassed it. If he was brutally honest, no one had even come close.

Shaking off that disturbing realization, he said, "So tell me, how did you and…what's his name?"

"Greg."

"How'd you two meet?"

"He's an attorney. We met at a house closing."

"How long ago?"

"Eight months."

"Is it serious?" He congratulated himself on his light tone, which was in such total contrast to the inexplicable tensing of his every muscle while he waited for her reply.

She tapped the corner of her mouth with her napkin, pushed her empty plate to the side, then reached for the manila envelope. "I'll let you know after he sees these," she said with a teasing wink.

What the hell kind of answer was that? Surely if they were serious, she'd have just said yes. Yet, he couldn't see her posing for such sensual photos for a man she didn't have deep feelings for. Still…she hadn't said yes, they were serious.

A flicker of something that felt suspiciously like hope flared to life in his chest, a tiny flame that he could neither blow out nor ignore. What was he—insane? He didn't want her to be available. If she was available, that would totally screw up his travel plans. Again.

Wouldn't it?

Hell, yeah.

Hell, no.

Why would it? If she was available, they could have a fling. *She is not a fling sort of woman,* his inner voice said. Totally true. Mallory was a forever sort of woman.

Which would be crappy timing because he was not currently a forever sort of guy. No, sir. Not him. He was footloose, worry free, Bachelor Number One, on his way to Europe for his dream vacation. She craved stability and for the next three months he'd be living out of a suitcase. Hell, in six months he wouldn't have a place to live. For all he knew, he might very well be running a tiki bar in Hawaii. So yeah, it was good she had a boyfriend. Yup, sure was. So he just needed to put all these crazy thoughts out of his head. Now.

Forcing himself to remain silent so as not to bombard her with more questions about her relationship, Adam ate his last onion ring and watched her look over the proofs, noting the flush that crept up her face. He tried to recall the last time he'd seen a woman blush and realized it was exactly one week ago. While he'd taken Mallory's pictures.

The urge to reach out and brush his fingers over that enticing wash of color gripped him, and he wrapped his hands around his frosty shake glass to keep from doing so. Unfortunately the chill did nothing to cool the heat nipping at him.

After taking a long, cold, chocolaty sip, he said, "You're blushing."

A self-conscious-sounding laugh escaped her. "It's just kind of embarrassing that you've seen me in my lingerie."

Mallory in her lingerie... Good God, he wasn't going to survive this. He unobtrusively shifted to lessen the growing discomfort in his Levi's. "At the risk of sounding crass, which is certainly not my intention, I've, um, seen you in less." And damn it, the image those words brought to mind did nothing to lessen his discomfort.

Her blush deepened. "Right—almost a decade ago. While we were..."

"Sleeping together?" some devil inside him made him say when she seemed at a loss for words.

"As I recall, sleep had little to do with it."

Touché. Damn, he felt as if he'd backed into a blowtorch. "Very little," he agreed, his voice tight.

"Well, that was a long time ago. This is different. And in these pictures, I look so..."

"Sexy?"

Her gaze shot up to his. "You think so?"

He mentally shook his head at the genuine questioning confusion in her eyes. "Hell, yes. Don't you?"

"Well...yeah, I suppose. I'm just not used to seeing myself this way."

"Believe me, Mallory, you have nothing to be embarrassed about."

She studied the photos for several more seconds, then said, "You did a really good job."

"Thanks. But it had nothing to do with me and everything to do with the subject matter. I blew up the three I thought were the best into eight-by-tens. My favorite's the last one."

She looked at the prints, staring the longest at the last one, then raised her gaze to his. "Why do you like this one the best?"

Because when I took it, I fantasized that you were thinking of me. Remembering me. Us. How good we were together. Because I was remembering you. "I think it really captures you. Your many facets. I like your expression, the contrasts it shows. You look seductive, yet shy. Tempting, playful, yet there's an air of innocence. I like the way your eyes are looking right into the camera. The way you seem to be saying, 'I want you more than Hershey's Kisses'—is that still your favorite candy, by the way?"

"Absolutely. I'll be forever loyal to my Kisses."

Eye on the ball, dude—don't think about kisses. He nodded. "As I was saying, 'I want you more than Hershey's Kisses.' Believe me, it's a look that any guy would give a *lot* to inspire." *Me, for example.*

The thought ambushed him and he had to clear his throat to locate his voice. "And the way your lips are slightly parted, just enough to issue an invitation, but not too much. You look great in all the pictures, but speaking as a guy, that one is guaranteed to knock his socks off." *It sure as hell knocked off mine.*

She looked back down at the print and frowned. "I hope you're right," she murmured.

Adam's eyebrows shot up at her softly spoken words, words that, based on her faraway expression, he wasn't sure she even realized she'd said. Christ, if one look at that photo of her didn't give George, or Greg, or whatever the hell his name was, an instant hard-on, the guy needed to check his pulse.

But her murmured words... Was it possible that all wasn't perfect between her and what's-his-name? If there was trouble in paradise... He pulled in a slow breath, and even though he fought it, a bit more kindling was tossed onto that internal fire, burning bright within him that-which-suspiciously-felt-like...

Hope.

She glanced at her watch. "I'm afraid I need to get going." She looked beyond him, over his shoulder, clearly looking for their waitress.

Disappointment washed through him, a fact that annoyed him. It was definitely time for this torturous stroll down memory lane to end. "You can go," he said. "I've got the check."

"You don't have to—"

"I *want* to. For old times' sake. Besides, I have to stick around and order something to-go for Nick."

"All right. Thank you." She slid toward the edge of the vinyl booth. "Lunch was delicious."

He rose then patted his stomach. "Sure was." He nodded toward the envelope. "Let us know which of the proofs you want made into prints."

"I will." She stood, looking a bit uncertain, as if she

didn't know whether to shake his hand or kiss his cheek or what. He helped her out by leaning forward and brushing his lips lightly against her smooth cheek. For a brief second, his eyes involuntarily closed. God, she smelled incredible. Like flowers in sunshine. He felt her lips touch his cheek, then she stepped back. "It was nice seeing you again."

"You, too." Really nice. Far too nice. Which meant that he needed to let her just walk out the door. But that stupid flame still burned, so instead he found himself saying lightly, "Maybe we can manage not to lose touch this time."

Instead of smiling and agreeing, a small frown furrowed between her brows. Then she flashed a quick smile that didn't quite reach her eyes. "Maybe," she said in a tone that made the word sound more like *I don't think so.* "But with all your traveling and the summer being my busiest time…"

Her voice trailed off and he swallowed a sensation that felt like disappointment but was surely really relief—especially as it irrevocably extinguished that ridiculous flame. He knew a kiss-off when he heard one—especially from this particular woman. Obviously he'd misread her and everything was fine between her and the boyfriend.

Really, he *was* relieved. Given his apparent strong attraction to her, seeing her again wouldn't be wise.

"I understand," he said, forcing a smile. "Here's hoping you sell a bazillion houses."

"That would be nice. Good luck with all your travels and finding a new career and a new place to live."

"Thanks." Unable to stop himself, he said, "And hey, if things don't work out with George—"

"Greg."

"Right. Give me a call." He gave her a jaunty salute and shot her his best lighthearted wink. "I'll treat you to another bacon cheeseburger."

"I'll keep that in mind."

She turned to go, and even though his inner voice warned him to remain silent, he found himself saying, "Six."

She turned back, clearly puzzled. "Six? What does that mean?"

"That's the number of times we made love that afternoon on the boat."

She said nothing for several long seconds, the silence swelling between them, tense and thick. Then she murmured, "Goodbye, Adam," and quickly wove her way through the labyrinth of tables.

He watched her walk away, his insides aching with a hollow sense of loss he wished like hell he didn't feel.

When she reached the door, she glanced back over her shoulder. They stared at each other and he wondered if she could see the desire he suspected lingered in his eyes. Seconds later she exited, then turned the corner and was lost to his sight.

Yeah, she was gone.

Unfortunately, he suspected the memories of her would linger in his mind for a long, long time.

4

MALLORY STOOD in the parking lot at her real-estate agent's office and waved goodbye to her clients, the Langdons. The afternoon house showing had gone extremely well and the couple had made an offer on the Maple Drive split-level. Matching up the Langdons and their three school-age children with the spacious house with the big backyard situated on a quiet cul-de-sac had filled her with a deep sense of satisfaction.

For Mallory, uniting a buyer with the perfect place to live involved much more than just showing them a *house*—it was about finding them a *home*. In a neighborhood that suited their lifestyle. She accomplished that by talking in depth to her customers, asking them lots of questions, and really listening to their responses. The Langdons' new home was only a short walk to the elementary school, and the school district was among the highest rated in the county. It was convenient to both shopping and the Long Island Railroad, which Mr. Langdon rode daily into Manhattan.

Entering the office, she spent some time trying to

catch up on paperwork, but her efforts were thwarted when her mind kept wandering…to the same thing it had kept wandering to for the past week.

Adam Clayton.

She squeezed her eyes shut to banish him from her mind, but instead an image of him flashed behind her eyelids. And not just any image. No, a memory of him naked. In the shower. They'd driven to Philadelphia to attend a concert and had spent the night at a cheap motel. It was the first time they'd spent an entire night together. First time they'd made love in the shower. She could visualize him so clearly…rivulets of warm water meandering down his muscular and aroused body. His eyes dark with desire. Holding out his hand in an invitation to join him. Slick, soapy hands, wet bodies aroused, his slow glide deep inside her—

Her eyes popped open and a disgusted sound pushed past her lips. Good grief, what was *wrong* with her? This had to stop. Dwelling on thoughts of Adam, indulging in reliving memories of their affair, was accomplishing nothing except filling her with a deep sense of guilt. And unfulfilled sexual frustration.

Surely the only reason she couldn't exorcise thoughts of Adam from her mind was that Greg had been away on a business trip to L.A. all week and she'd been lonely.

Hadn't she been lonely?

"Yes, of course," she said out loud to the empty room. "Loneliness, missing Greg—that's been the source of my frustration and discontent."

But the words roused her conscience, which forced

her to admit that she'd actually enjoyed having a week to herself. Enjoyed not worrying about meshing her crowded schedule with Greg's insane calendar. Enjoyed spending her evenings in peaceful silence, catching up on her reading. Cooking simple meals for herself or just ordering in. Hanging out in ratty old clothes.

Greg didn't really enjoy quiet evenings at home. He preferred elegant meals at upscale restaurants. While Mallory definitely liked that once in a while, she also liked grabbing a pizza and popping a movie into the DVD player. Or just curling up with a good book. Greg liked being on the go. Driving into Manhattan to check out the latest club, bar or restaurant. Again—all fun, but she was definitely a girl who needed and enjoyed her downtime and beauty sleep, whereas Greg thrived on only four or five hours of shut-eye a night.

They usually got together two or three nights a week, then again on Saturday or Sunday evening. Greg complained that she worked all day on the weekends, but hey—she was a Realtor. Those were her two busiest days. Recently, on the odd evening she managed to talk him into staying in, he invariably ended up bored and channel surfing.

Of course, it hadn't been that way when they'd first met. No, then he hadn't minded so much staying in, and their sex life had been very good. Well, okay, it had been *good.* Oh, all right, it had been *adequate.* But Greg was a decent, intelligent, hardworking, attractive guy who'd persistently pursued her and she was willing to put in some time and effort to see where the relationship might—or might not—go. He was steady and stable.

Dependable. He owned his own house. Had worked for the same law firm for the past ten years. Didn't want to live anywhere other than Long Island. Wanted to raise a family here.

Not that they'd talked about marriage yet, but the subject would have to be addressed eventually. Not too long ago she'd considered broaching the future, but over the last few months, things hadn't been going all that well. Greg hadn't been as attentive, and quite frankly, neither had she. He'd been traveling to Los Angeles frequently, a couple of times spending the weekend there. Their sex life had, in her opinion, declined from adequate to perfunctory.

Which had led her to Picture This. Which had led her to Adam. Unfortunate timing as he was the guy who'd set the bar for her sexual expectations—set it so high, no other man had ever come close. Which had led to a really confusing week where the more she tried not to think of her former lover, the more he invaded her thoughts. Which surely would change as soon as she saw Greg again and showed him the photos. Yes, surely that would get them back on track and light a fire beneath both of them. She wasn't a quitter and wasn't about to give up on a decent guy without trying simply because they'd hit a rough spot.

She and Greg had spoken over the phone several times this past week, but the time difference to the West Coast made it difficult to keep in touch daily. He was flying home tomorrow and they were meeting for dinner. She couldn't wait to show him his present....

Her gaze drifted to the manila envelope on her desk.

Unable to stop herself, she reached out. After opening the envelope, she slid out the photos and studied them carefully. And with each photo her discomfort and guilt increased.

Adam had said she looked sexy, and she couldn't deny that she agreed. Sexy and…aroused. Which she'd definitely been. Which is precisely how she'd hoped to look.

Only problem was that it wasn't thoughts of Greg that had inspired her arousal. It was memories of Adam.

"Argh!" She pressed her fingers to her temples in a fruitless attempt to change the direction of her thoughts then slipped the photos back into the envelope, where she couldn't see them taunting her, whispering, *Adam is the one you were posing for. Whose hands and lips and tongue you imagined touching your body.*

Damn it, just as she'd feared, having lunch with him today had been a *bad* idea. An exercise in futility that had sorely tested her self-control. The effort she'd expended not to touch him, to keep her thoughts on track, to suppress the memories of their affair, to resist the urge to delve more deeply into his personal life, had left her frustrated and emotionally exhausted.

She absolutely shouldn't have spent any more time with him—time that had only fueled more memories and fantasies. When his lips had brushed her fingertips while taking a bite of her onion ring, the vivid images pounding through her brain had stolen her breath. How many hours had they spent feeding each other? Everything from grapes to Hershey's Kisses to French fries. It had become a game, a form of foreplay that had always ended with them making love. Feeding him today had resulted in a bolt of lust that had practically incinerated her. It had required all her willpower to hide her reaction, and she wasn't certain she'd succeeded.

Then, when they'd parted, that light kiss on the cheek...

Her eyes slid closed and she instantly recalled how great he smelled. Clean, with just a hint of fresh-smelling soap. He'd never cared for wearing cologne, and clearly his preference hadn't changed. She recalled how she used to love burying her face in the deliciously warm spot where his neck and shoulder met and just breathe him in.

Opening her eyes, she sighed. His suggestion that they stay in touch had hit her with the cold, wet washcloth of reality. Definitely not a good idea. Especially since she'd wanted so badly to agree—a fact that only made her feel more guilty and disloyal toward Greg. She'd demurred, but the effort had cost her. As it had cost her to walk away after he'd weakened her knees with that single word: *six*.

A heated flush engulfed her. He'd remembered they'd made love six times that afternoon on the boat. And God help her, she'd never forgotten.

Her cell phone rang, yanking her from her thoughts, and she dug the flip phone from her handbag. Her caller ID informed her it was Kellie. Before Mallory could so much as say hello, her best friend said, "Okay, out with it. How'd the pictures come out?"

Mallory's glance cut to the manila envelope. "Surprisingly well."

"Where are you now?"

"At the office."

"Good. Stay there. I'm only a few minutes away. Bye."

Mallory closed her phone, then, determined to concentrate on work until Kellie arrived, spent the next ten minutes pulling up new home listings in the area on her computer. She didn't look up until the front door opened.

Kellie Straton walked into the office with the bubbly enthusiasm of a teenager. Dressed in cutoffs and a tank top over a neon-pink bathing suit, her honey-blond hair pulled back into a haphazard ponytail and designer sunglasses resting on top of her head, she looked cool and perky—or at least as cool and perky as one could be during a July heat wave.

"Off to the beach?" Mallory asked.

"Absolutely. It's the only place to be on a beastly day like this."

"And what about Kellie's Korner?" she asked, referring to the funky clothing-and-jewelry boutique Kellie owned in the center of town.

"The air-conditioning unit broke down during lunch and the repairman can't come until Monday. I stayed open for a couple hours, but when it became too hot inside, I closed up shop."

"Sorry to hear about the air-conditioning."

"Me, too. But business was slow anyway. So c'mon. I have an extra bathing suit in my bag," she said, patting the huge bright green terry-cloth satchel hanging on her shoulder. "You can change here and come with me. I'll look at your pictures while I wait."

"Wish I could, but I still have work here."

Kellie made a *tsking* sound. "You know, this 'all work, no play' is turning you into a dull girl."

Mallory cocked a brow and slid the envelope toward her friend. "Dull, you say? Take a look at these and tell me if you still think I'm dull."

Kellie slid out the photos and Mallory had the satisfaction of seeing her friend's eyes widen. "Holy smoke, Mal. These are *hot*." She plopped down into a chair and studied the sheets closely. "The photographer did an excellent job of capturing your inner sexiness. I think I might have to schedule an appointment and have some of these babies taken."

An unpleasant sensation she absolutely refused to examine prowled through Mallory at the thought of Kellie posing for Adam. After a quick inner debate, Mallory decided to share the details. "The photographer did a *really* excellent job, considering he's a stockbroker."

Kellie looked up. "Huh?"

After pulling in a bracing breath, she quickly told Kellie her history with Adam. When she finished, Kellie folded her arms across her chest and tapped her pink flip-flop on the hardwood floor. "We've known each other for *four years* and you've never mentioned this guy?"

"I guess I just kept him in the past—where he belonged."

"And *now* you've waited an entire week to tell me you saw him again?" she asked, sounding both miffed and hurt. "What's up with that?"

"I'm sorry," Mallory said, twisting her fingers together. "Really. I've honestly wanted to talk to you about it, but we've both been busy and I just didn't… know what to say," she finished lamely.

"So what's this Adam Clayton like now?" Kellie asked.

"He's…the same."

Kellie shook her head. "Uh-uh. No way. No guy is the same at thirty as he was at twenty. Either he's worse, as in his six-pack abs are now a keg and he's losing his hair, or he's better—more rugged and manly, with an air of some experience about him. So which one is it?"

Mallory plopped into the chair opposite Kellie and huffed out a long sigh. "More rugged and manly."

"Uh-huh. Based on these pictures, I figured as much." Kellie studied her for several seconds then reached out and clasped her hand. "I'm guessing you've been thinking about him this entire last week?"

"Can't get him out of my mind," Mallory admitted with a defeated, humorless smile.

"I can see you're upset, Mal, but hey—it's not a crime to reminisce about the past. Or to think another guy is attractive. The world is littered with gorgeous men. Believe me, I know. I see their pictures in *People* magazine all the time."

Mallory attempted a weak grin. "Yeah, but half of what's going through my mind is X-rated."

"Half—or more like three-quarters? 'Cause I don't think it really constitutes a problem unless it's at least three-quarters."

"The problem is that for the past week, thoughts of

Adam filled my mind ninety-nine percent of the time. Didn't leave much time for Greg—you know, the guy I'm supposed to be thinking about. I just feel confused and disloyal and guilty as hell."

"Maybe this is a sign that you and Greg are coming to the end of the line. There's been trouble on your horizon for a while now."

Mallory wanted to refute Kellie's words, but she couldn't. After all, wasn't taking the sexy photos an effort to try to fix what was wrong between her and Greg? "I know, but these pictures were supposed to *help* with the problems—not cause more." She shook her head, feeling lost and confused and not liking it one bit. "Maybe we are coming to the end, but I won't know unless I give it my best shot. Greg has his faults, but he's a good man. Steady. Stable. Dependable. You know how important that is to me. And you know how unsuccessful I've been in my attempt to find a guy who wants more than a fling. Who isn't a slacker or a jerk or unemployed or up to his ears in debt or—" She shook her head. "You get my point. Greg has his faults, but who doesn't? God knows I have plenty. I'm just not willing to give up on us without trying."

"Well, if those photos don't resuscitate your relationship, it's totally flatlined. You're seeing Greg tomorrow night?"

"Yes. I'll call you Monday to let you know how it goes."

"Good. I'll forgive you once for holding out on me for a week, but not twice."

"Gotcha."

Looking unusually serious, Kellie studied her for several seconds. "You know, Mal, it kinda sounds to me like Adam's 'The One Who Got Away.'"

Mallory considered, then shrugged. "I suppose he could be called that, but what difference does it make? The operative words are 'Who Got Away.'"

"No. The operative words are 'The One.'"

The One. That seemed to reverberate through Mallory's mind along with an image of Adam. Then she shook her head. "That's ridiculous."

"No, it's not. It's statistically a fact. I just read an article about this in *Metro Chick* magazine. Eighty-eight percent of women who hook up again with 'The One Who Got Away' discover that he's 'The One.' *Eighty-eight percent,* Mallory."

"Which means that twelve percent discover that they'd have been better off if they'd let him remain 'Away.'"

"When did you become such a pessimist?"

"I'm not a pessimist. I'm a realist. A realist who already has a boyfriend."

"And if you didn't?"

Mallory's heart tripped over itself. If she didn't have a boyfriend... *You'd be all over Adam Clayton like sparkle on diamonds and you damn well know it,* her inner voice informed her.

Apparently her expression gave her away, because Kellie nodded. "Figured as much."

"But...but Adam is all wrong for me," Mallory blurted out. "*All* wrong." There. She'd said it—twice. A few dozen more reminders and that would convince her. Probably. "He was wrong for me before and he's wrong for me now."

"How?"

"Timing issues. The reason we split up before was because we were heading in opposite directions, and we're doing the exact same thing now. I'm looking for permanency. Stability. To expand my career, take on more responsibility, and enjoy my new house. He's currently unemployed, doesn't know what sort of new career he wants, is living the bachelor lifestyle, and plans to travel the globe, no doubt indulging in flings in every time zone—and has no idea where he plans to live once his lease is up. He even mentioned opening a tiki bar in Hawaii. Stable and permanent that is not. I'm focused on business and my future, and he's Mr. Margaritaville."

"He's not going to be unemployed forever, Mal. Besides, if he sold a seat on the stock exchange, he's not hurting for money. He has time to decide what he wants to do next. And as for the tiki bar and him doing his bachelor thing, nothing says you have to *marry* the guy. You could just be his Eastern Standard time-zone fling."

Mallory briefly tipped back her head and squeezed her eyes shut. "You're not helping, you know. You're *supposed* to say, 'The only reason you're thinking about Adam is because his reappearance in your life caught you off guard and swamped you with nostalgia. Now that there's no reason to see him again, you'll forget him. Greg's your boyfriend. Think about him.'"

"I'm not at all convinced that's what I'm supposed to be saying, but I hate seeing you so unraveled. So I'll play it your way." A devilish grin curved Kellie's lips.

"Forget your sexy former lover and focus on, uh, what's his face."

"Thanks. Very helpful."

"Always glad to be of service." Again her friend's gaze turned serious. "Mal, do you love Greg?"

A humorless laugh escaped her. "Ah, the question I've asked myself at least a dozen times in the past week."

"And your answer?"

Mallory let out a long, slow breath. "Honestly? I just don't know. And after eight months of dating, I think I *should* know. I want—need—to discover the answer. But it isn't fair to either me or Greg if I let an accidental encounter with a past lover influence me. I need to decide based strictly on what Greg and I have—or don't have—together. He's the first decent man I've met in a long time and I don't want to make a mistake by throwing it all away too soon."

Kellie gave her hand a commiserating squeeze. "That's very wise. Just keep in mind that if another man can arouse strong feelings in you, maybe your feelings for Greg aren't as deep as you might have thought."

"Good advice. How much do I owe you for the consult, doc?"

"I'll send you a bill. Sure I can't talk you into coming to the beach?"

"No thanks. I want to clear off my desk."

They both stood, and after exchanging a quick hug, Kellie left. Mallory took a deep breath and forced everything into perspective. These crazy thoughts about

Adam were nothing more than a blip on her emotional radar. A bad case of nostalgia run amok. As soon as she saw Greg again, rekindled their sex life, everything would fall back into place.

Feeling better, she spent the next hour clearing away items from her in-box, then decided to call it a day. The evening stretched out before her like an undisturbed swath of virgin beach—tranquil, peaceful and deserted. With no one to please but herself. With that in mind, she decided to indulge in Thai food, which Greg hated, and pick up a chick flick from Blockbuster. *Ooooh. A hot night. Shine on, you wild and crazy diamond,* her inner voice snickered.

After gathering her things, she left the office, locking the door behind her. Suffocating heat radiated up from the parking lot blacktop and she quickened her pace to her car. Once the air-conditioning cooled off the interior, she headed out of the lot toward Blockbuster. After selecting her movie, she drove on toward the Thai Palace. On the way there, she detoured down the side street where Greg lived to check on his house as she usually did when he went away for a week at a time. Even though he stopped his newspaper and mail deliveries, unsolicited flyers were often tossed onto driveways. Since such things lying around were red flags that no one was home, Mallory had made it a habit to cut down his street to make sure everything looked undisturbed.

Her eyebrows shot upward a block away from the small brick ranch when she spotted what looked like Greg's silver Lexus parked in the driveway. Seconds later, she pulled in behind what was most definitely his car. Obviously he'd taken an earlier flight.

But why hadn't he called her? Probably he'd caught the red-eye and was catching up on some sleep. Hmm… if that was the case, maybe he'd like a little company in his bed. No time like the present to put in that extra effort she'd been talking about and rekindling their sex life.

Armed with the manila envelope inside her oversize purse and with a smile playing around her lips, she used the key he'd given her to unlock the door. She stepped into the small ceramic-tiled foyer and closed the door behind her. The sound of soft jazz poured from the stereo. Because of the way the house was laid out, she could immediately see that Greg wasn't in either the den or eat-in kitchen, so she headed down the carpeted hallway toward his bedroom. Not wanting to wake him—at least not until she slid between the sheets next to him—she quietly opened his bedroom door.

Well, there certainly wasn't any need to worry about waking him up—he was clearly wide-awake. And no need to worry about rekindling his sex life—his was apparently just fine. Nor did she need to think that he might like a little company in his bed—he already had plenty. In the form of a naked buxom blonde who was riding him like he was the lead horse in the freakin' Kentucky Derby. Beneath the blonde, Greg groaned, his hands filled to overflowing with the woman's melon-size breasts.

Mallory's heavy leather purse slid off her shoulder and hit the floor with a resounding splat. Her jaw, she was certain, joined her purse less than a second later.

Greg and Blondie turned toward her. Then they, too, froze. Blondie, who appeared to be about nineteen, looked surprised and annoyed at the interruption. Greg looked shocked and all the color drained from his face.

"Who the hell are you?" Blondie asked, all *Cosmo*-girl attitude.

Mallory had to swallow twice to locate her voice. When she found it, it was accompanied by a tidal wave of anger. "I'd ask you the same thing, but there's no need since it's pretty obvious."

The blonde flipped her hair and heaved a put-upon sigh. "Listen, I know I look just like Pam Anderson, but I'm not her."

While a bark of incredulous, humorless laughter escaped Mallory, Greg muttered a round of curses and rolled Blondie off him. Blondie didn't take too kindly to that, however, and promptly rolled to her knees and slammed her hands onto her hips. Mallory, still shocked into immobility, dimly noted that the woman not only had an obvious boob job, but she wasn't a natural blonde.

Way more than she needed to know. Definitely time to get the hell out of this den of horrors. After snatching up her purse, she turned, then walked swiftly down the hallway on shaking legs toward the front door.

"Mallory, wait," came Greg's voice, followed by more curses, then a terse "Stay here"—presumably to Blondie.

She quickened her pace and had just opened the door when he grabbed her arm. Mallory whipped around and skewered him with a look, and, if looks could cut throats, he'd have bled all over his white ceramic tiles. Her gaze flicked down, noting he was still naked. And obviously startled.

"Take your hand off me. *Now.* Unless you want a new career singing soprano for the Vienna Boys' Choir."

He instantly released her. "Mallory, listen to me. This—"

"Isn't what it looks like?"

"No, it's not."

She debated smacking him upside his cheating head with her purse but quickly discarded the idea. Her purse was heavy enough to put him in traction and, tempting as that sounded, he wasn't worth being charged with assault over. Instead she crossed her arms over her chest and adopted an exaggerated stunned expression.

"You mean this *isn't* a case of me walking in while you were boffing some bimbo? Then do enlighten me. I'm *all* agog to hear."

Color washed into his pale face. "I can't stand it when you're sarcastic."

"My heart's bleeding for you. Really. And if I had another six hours to waste on you, I'd be delighted to tell you all the things I can't stand about you."

His flush deepened. "I know this looks like I just picked up some woman, but it's not that way. I met Mandy three months ago, and, well, we've fallen in love. I had every intention of telling you tomorrow that I'd met someone else."

"Really? Before or after you bought her a Happy Meal?"

"She's not that much younger than me, damn it. She's twenty."

"How perfect that her age and IQ match."

He had the gall to look pissed at *her*. "I'll have you know," he said stiffly, "she hopes to be a lawyer some-day."

"Right. And in the meanwhile, she'll just screw law-yers. You two are perfect for each other." She yanked open the front door. He moved as if he meant to grab her arm again and she shot him a look that could have incinerated raw meat.

"What about my stuff that's at your place?" Greg asked. "Can I come over tomorrow and get it?"

Mallory couldn't help but laugh. "Jeez, you've really got balls." Her gaze flicked down to his crotch. "Hmm. Maybe not. Anyway, I don't want you, or your stuff, in my house. I'll box everything up and send it to you."

"All right. I'll do the same for you." His eyes nar-rowed. "You won't wreck my clothes or CDs, will you?"

"Clearly I need to point out that *I* am not the one be-having badly here. Besides, I wouldn't waste my time or energy. I would, however, ask for your key to my house." She started removing his house key from her ring.

"Fine." He stalked down the hallway toward his bedroom.

"Do us both a favor and put on some pants," she said sweetly.

He entered the bedroom and Mallory heard Blondie ask, "Who the hell is she and what the hell is going on?"

Mallory cleared her throat then called out loudly,

"As for who the hell I am—I'm the girlfriend he's had for the past eight months. He says he was going to tell me about you tomorrow, so maybe that's when he was also going to tell you about me." Mallory paused and smiled grimly at Melon Boobs's gasp. "As for what the hell's going on," she continued, "Jerk-off's putting on some pants, thank God, and getting me the key to my house, which I'd given him. As soon as it's in my hand, he's all yours."

Seconds later Greg strode from the bedroom—wearing pants, thank God—his expression resembling a thundercloud. Melon Boobs followed close on his heels, her ample assets barely covered by Greg's dress shirt.

Mallory held out her hand and Greg slapped her key into it. She then dropped his key into his outstretched palm.

Melon Boobs shot Mallory a nasty glare. "He was all mine *before* he gave you back your key, honey."

"Uh-huh. And what a prize he is." Mallory shook her head. "You know, Candy—"

"Mandy," the young woman said through clenched teeth.

"—I actually feel sorry for you. This guy has proven himself to be nothing more than a lying, cheating bottom-feeder. I'm thinking you can do better. I *know* I can. But he's your problem now. I wish you both luck."

Without a backward glance, she sailed through the doorway and quickly entered her car. *Just get away, just get away,* her inner voice chanted. At the end of the block, well out of sight of Greg's house, she pulled into

the strip mall on the corner and immediately parked at
the far end of the lot, in front of an Italian bakery. Then
she leaned her head back against the headrest, closed
her eyes and forced herself to take slow, deep breaths.

Good God, she was shaking. And even though she
tried to will them away, hot tears leaked from beneath
her eyelids and trailed down her cheeks. Damn it, she
did *not* want to cry. She shoved the wetness aside with
impatient fingers, but a fresh onslaught of tears spilled
over.

Had she ever been this angry? This humiliated? If so,
she couldn't recall. But she was more than angry—she
was furious. At him. And herself. And that snarky,
melon-boobed bimbo. But mostly him.

That *bastard!* He'd not only cheated on her, he'd
been cheating on her for *months.* How mortifying and
degrading was *that?*

But then anger at herself boiled over, washing everything else aside. *This* was the guy she'd believed steady?
Stable? Dependable? How could she have been so stupid? So blind? Such a sap? So willing to go that extra
mile to try to fix things between them? Even going so
far as having those boudoir photos taken? Well, thank
God she'd discovered the truth before she'd humiliated
herself further by giving him those.

At the thought of the pictures, an image of Adam rose
behind her closed eyes, pushing a humorless laugh past
her tight throat. How ironic that she'd felt so guilty
about her attraction to Adam. Obviously she hadn't
needed to worry.

Keeping her eyes closed, she sat perfectly still for

several minutes, concentrating on her relaxing breathing techniques while gathering her scattered thoughts. When the tears stopped flowing and her heart rate had settled and she felt calmer, she took a detailed emotional inventory.

Angry? Oh, yeah. Humiliated? Check. Self-disgust for being a trusting fool? Yup. Relieved?

Yes.

Her eyes popped open and she pulled the clip from her hair then tunneled her hands through the strands. Blowing out a long, slow breath, she continued. Hurt?

Nope.

Heartbroken?

No way.

And that irrevocably answered the "did she love Greg" question she hadn't been able to answer earlier. Obviously she didn't for if she did, she'd be devastated and brokenhearted instead of pissed. Which told her exactly how lucky she was to be rid of him. With her new twenty-twenty hindsight guiding her, she clearly saw that they'd been heading toward the end for months. Yes, it was a shame she'd given the relationship more time than it deserved, but she didn't have to give it, or him, another thought.

Still, even though he hadn't crushed her heart, there unfortunately was still something about getting dumped for a not-even-old-enough-to-legally-drink Playboy-centerfold type that was pretty damaging to the ego. Damn. Her heart didn't need a boost, but her trampled self-esteem definitely did.

She considered calling Kellie, who she knew would

happily spend the evening wallowing in an "I can't believe that ass dumped such a great girl" Greg-bashing party, but that wasn't what her bruised ego craved. And a rented movie and Thai takeout wouldn't do the trick, either.

No, her wounded pride demanded that she feel desirable. Wanted. Attractive. Sexy.

And she knew exactly the man for the job.

5

ADAM SAT BEHIND the computer at Picture This and typed in order number after order number, slowly working his way through the stack of invoices piled on Nick's desk. For every big party, such as a wedding, at least four hundred proofs were taken. Each proof was numbered and from them various-size prints and albums were made up for the bride and groom, their families and friends. Based on the number of invoices and orders in the in-box, Nick's business was booming. Weddings, anniversary parties, christenings, bar mitzvahs, sweet sixteens, graduations, private sittings—with more jobs being booked every day.

He'd just completed another invoice when a light tapping sound had him looking up and he stilled—except for his heart, which seemed to stumble over itself.

Mallory stood outside the front glass door, which Adam had locked when Nick left an hour earlier. He jumped to his feet and strode quickly across the tiled floor.

"Hi," he said, pulling the door inward. "C'mon in."

His smile faded when he saw her pale face and what looked like red-rimmed eyes. "You okay?"

"Yes," she said, brushing past him to enter. His body tensed at that brief contact and he pretended he hadn't felt it. Or caught a whiff of her light, flowery fragrance. Gritting his teeth, he kept his back to her and spent a few extra seconds relocking the door, telling himself to get a grip. He shouldn't be so thrown off balance just because she'd stopped by. Probably she just wanted some more prints made of her photos. For what's-his-name.

But when he turned around, she threw him off kilter again. She stood less than two feet away, looking at him with an expression he couldn't read, but one that set his blood on fire. And then she blew him right out of the water by stepping forward, pressing herself against him and tunneling her fingers through his hair. Then she lifted up on her toes, pulled his head toward hers and kissed him. Like she meant it.

If all the blood hadn't instantly drained from his head to settle in his groin, most likely he would have wondered what had brought this on. But anything that involved thinking was going to have to wait. His arms went around her, pulling her closer, tighter against him, and he deepened the kiss she'd initiated.

She tasted exactly as he remembered. Delicious. Warm, sweet and seductive. Like melted chocolate. And felt exactly the same in his arms. Soft and curvy and feminine. A perfect fit. The erotic sensation of her tongue rubbing against his drove everything from his mind except for one single word that pounded through him with growing urgency.

More.

But before he could act upon it, she shifted gears again by breaking off their kiss. Splaying her hands against his chest, right over the spot where his heart was frantically trying to play catch-up, she leaned back in the circle of his arms. He noted with some satisfaction that her breathing sounded as labored as his. And she looked as bamboozled as he felt.

Surely some words were called for, but with his liquefied brain still engulfed in a steamy fog of lust, speech was beyond him.

Her palms glided over his chest, shooting another arrow of fiery want directly downward. His hands, which rested on her hips and kept her firmly anchored against him, involuntarily tightened.

"Figured as much," she said in a voice that sounded like rough velvet.

There was no doubt what she meant—that the heat they'd just generated came as no surprise to her—but damn, he was impressed she could form a coherent sentence. He wasn't there yet, so he just nodded. At least he thought he nodded. He meant to.

"I was afraid you might have already left. I'm glad you were still here."

He swallowed twice and managed to find his voice. "Yeah. Me, too." Damn glad.

But then his gaze searched her face, confirming what he'd thought he'd seen before she'd deep-fried all his synapses. His gut clenched at the sight of her red-rimmed, slightly swollen eyes and coherency returned with a thump. "You've been crying."

"How do you know that?"

He lifted one hand and gently brushed a fingertip under her eye. "Through a wondrous process called 'sight.'" And given the way she'd greeted him, there was no doubt in his mind that whatever was wrong had to do with her boyfriend. "What happened?"

She gently pushed against his chest and he let her go, watching in silence while she put several feet between them and drew a deep breath. Then she offered him a half smile that didn't touch her eyes. "You told me that if things didn't work out with Greg, I should give you a call. Since I was in the neighborhood, I thought I'd stop by instead."

Just as he'd thought. A breakup with the boyfriend. While he couldn't deny part of him was glad, he hated to see the evidence that she'd cried. And even as his heart pounded with anticipation, his common sense issued a stern warning to proceed with caution. Clearly she'd had a fight with what's-his-name. While Adam was glad she'd turned to him and he was happy to offer his friendship, he didn't relish getting caught in the crossfire and left bleeding should she and the boyfriend make up.

After firmly telling his heart—and his fully aroused hormones—to chill out, he reached out and took her hand then led her toward the corner waiting area where a sofa, two comfy chairs and a coffee table were located. "Let's sit down for a minute." After she'd settled herself on the sofa, he pulled up one of the chairs to sit facing her. "Okay, tell me what happened."

She stared at her hands, which plucked at the handle

of her purse. "Do you know the three words you most don't want to hear while you're making love?" When he shook his head, she looked up and said, "Honey, I'm home."

A spurt of white-hot fury roared through Adam. The damn bastard had *cheated* on her. Not only did that infuriate him, but he could only shake his head in stunned disbelief. How could any guy possibly be so stupid? To have a woman like Mallory then lose her—

Hey, nine years ago you were that stupid guy, his inner voice reminded him.

Well, yeah, he'd been stupid—but out of fear. He sure as hell hadn't cheated on her. How could any guy who had Mallory in his bed want anyone else?

Reaching out, he clasped both her hands and squeezed. "I'm sorry something so hurtful happened to you, sweetheart."

"Thanks." She blew out slow breath. "It was a pretty shocking—and unappealing—sight, let me tell you. And the woman he was with…" She made an exclamation of disgust. "Give me a break. She's a twenty-year-old lawyer wannabe with badly bleached hair and a boob job that looks as if she used Velcro to stick two cantaloupes to her chest. They're *in luuuuuv.*" Her upper lip curled à la Elvis Presley. "You might want to move back. I think I'm gonna hack up a hair ball."

He brushed the pads of his thumbs over the soft backs of her hands. "I'll take my chances."

A sound that resembled a growl rumbled in her throat and she abruptly stood. Her hands slid from his and she paced in front of him. "I won't bore you with the details, but suffice it to say things weren't going all that well between me and Greg for the last few months. I blamed most of it on our hectic schedules, although I was coming to realize that we didn't have as much in common as I'd originally thought. And that those differences were really…irritating. Of course, I wasn't aware that there were three of us in the equation. I'm certainly glad I found out now as opposed to later."

"Did you…do you love him?"

She halted and turned to face him. "I wasn't sure exactly what my feelings were before, but now I am, and the answer is a definite no. But I cared for him. Enough to give the relationship some more time and effort. Still, there was always something lacking between us—especially recently. Of course, any caring I may have had is now well and truly extinguished. I just wish I didn't have the visual in my head of him and Melon Boobs together."

She resumed her pacing and he sat quietly, letting her gather her thoughts. Finally she continued, "It's not that I'm heartbroken. Far from it. I'm actually relieved. But damn it, I'm *angry*. At him for being such a lying cheat, but mostly at myself for hanging in there *way* too long. For believing he was the sort of stable, steady, dependable guy I was looking for. For being so stupid."

He snagged her hand as she walked by him, then rose to stand in front of her, biting down his own anger at the bastard who had made her feel this way. After lightly clasping her by the shoulders, he looked directly into her eyes and said, "You are not stupid, Mallory. You did nothing wrong."

"I was too trusting."

"You were lied to. That isn't in any way a reflection on *your* character. The fact that you were willing to go the extra mile for a relationship shows the sort of person you are. You're loyal. You have integrity. And you're not a quitter."

Her chin quivered and she gave him a shaky smile. "You're making me feel much better."

"I'm glad. But you *should* feel good. Even though the circumstances were crappy, look at it this way—you were just freed from a relationship that, based on the facts that you feel relieved and didn't love him, you obviously no longer wanted to be involved in anyway."

"You're right. I know. It's just that it's so *discouraging* to be tossed over for someone who looks as if she just breezed into town between Playboy centerfold modeling assignments."

"There's absolutely no reason for you to be discouraged. Clearly the guy is an ass. And supremely foolish. And unbelievably blind."

Unmistakable gratitude flickered in her eyes. "Well, thanks. I appreciate the outrage on my behalf. But jeez, the guy is a thirty-four-year-old Ivy League graduate. You'd think he'd at least have the sense, the taste to dump me for someone who's old enough to buy her own beer and who has more going for her than an enormous pair of fake knockers." She heaved a sigh. "But maybe she's very nice."

He tucked a stray silky dark curl behind her ear. "Not as nice as you."

"And really smart."

"Not as smart as you."

"Probably she's prettier than I thought—I wasn't exactly concentrating on her face."

"She couldn't possibly be prettier than you."

Her lips twitched. "You know, you're really doing an outstanding job soothing my wounded ego."

"Good." His gaze searched hers. "So that's what that kiss was about. An ego stroke."

A rosy blush stained her cheeks. "I guess I needed a little reassurance that I wasn't a troll." Doubt flickered in her eyes. "You're not angry with me, are you?"

"Angry? At being kissed by a gorgeous sexy woman? A kiss that made me feel like you'd tossed me into an oven and hit Broil? Hell, no. But surely it was obvious that anger was *not* my reaction at all." He cupped her face in his hands and stroked his thumbs over her smooth cheeks. "Consider me more than willing to give you all the reassurance you need."

Whoa, hold on there, dude, his inner voice yelled. *What are you saying? Have you forgotten why Mallory isn't right for you?*

No, he hadn't forgotten. He'd just…reassessed. Just because she was a "forever" sort of gal didn't mean she had to be *his* forever gal. Just because she was the kind of woman who *could* wreak havoc with a guy's travel plans, didn't mean he'd let her mess up *his* plans— again. If she wanted an ego-stroking fling, hell, who better for the job than Bachelor Number One?

Besides, it wasn't as if anything could come of this. He'd just be the rebound guy. Everybody knew Rebound Guy never ended up being permanent. Which, given the fact that he was leaving for Europe the day after tomorrow, made their timing perfect—a first for them.

"Hmm. Reassuring me…" she repeated. "I might just take you up on that offer."

"*Might?* I guess I'll just have to see what it'll take to change that 'might' into a definite." Another wash of color stole over her cheeks and he brushed his thumbs over that enticing blush. "Here's something that should help reassure you. Our lunch today? An exercise in torture. You have no idea the enormous amount of self-control it required not to touch you. Kiss you."

"You did touch me. You did kiss me."

"Not the way I wanted to."

The ghost of a smile flirted with the corners of her mouth. "I have to admit, I came here with the hope that you'd possibly be willing to give my wilted self-esteem a boost."

"Sweetheart, there is no *possibly* about how very willing I am." Shadows still lingered in her big brown eyes—shadows he wanted erased. His gaze dipped to her mouth and he barely squelched a groan of pure want. The need to kiss her was unbearable. Yet he wanted to do a hell of a lot more than kiss her. But for now…

Just one more kiss, he promised himself. *Just to reassure her of how incredibly desirable she is.*

His hands slipped from her face to draw her slowly into his arms. His heart pounded as if he'd run around the entire island of Manhattan. Lowering his head, he brushed his lips softly against hers. And instantly realized his mistake. Just one kiss would not be possible.

He feathered his lips over hers again, a whisper of reacquaintance that only begged for more. She responded by parting her lips and gliding the tip of her tongue over his bottom lip. And in a flash of fire he knew that one hundred kisses wouldn't be enough.

With a groan, he pulled her closer, tighter against him and slipped his tongue into the silky heat of her mouth. In a heartbeat he was lost, all sense of time and place overwhelmed by the need to touch. And taste. Her delicious feminine scent invaded his head and his rapidly vanishing control slipped another notch. One of his hands smoothed up her back to tangle in her soft hair, while the other hand skimmed lower to cup the luscious curve of her buttocks. And suddenly the years faded away and he was flooded with that same wild, reckless feeling she'd once inspired in him. When they couldn't keep their hands off each other. Couldn't get enough of each other.

Her arms tightened around his neck and she shifted against him. His erection jerked, and if his eyes had been opened, he knew they'd have glazed over. As it was, she had bells ringing in his head.

Breaking off their kiss, she gasped, "Phone."

Phone? A loud ringing permeated the haze of arousal surrounding him.

"Do you need to answer it?" she asked, nipping little kisses against his jaw.

He wanted to say no, but damn it, it might be Nick. "Yeah, I should," he said, reluctantly releasing her. He was so hard he couldn't walk without wincing. When he made it to the desk, he shot the phone a baleful glare at the interruption and snatched up the receiver.

"Picture This," he said, his voice coming out in a husky rasp.

"Adam, is that you?" asked Nick through the phone.

"It's me. What's up?" He looked down at the bulge behind his fly and hoped Nick wouldn't ask him the same question.

"You sound funny. You okay?"

"I'm fine." *Except for the strangulation occurring in the front of my jeans.* "How 'bout you?"

"Good. Listen, my neighbor just called asking if there was any free studio time next week, and since the schedule's on my desk there, I thought I'd take a chance and see if you were still around. Can you check it for me?"

"Sure." Adam opened the appointment book and flipped the pages. After rattling off the trio of openings, Nick picked one and asked that Adam write in his neighbor Audrey Shay's name. "Taken care of," Adam said, closing the book.

"Thanks, dude. See you tomorrow afternooon."

"Bye." Adam hung up the phone, then tunneled his hands through his hair. His gaze shifted to Mallory, who stood exactly where he'd left her in front of the sofa. His heart thumped at the arousal that still lurked in her eyes, and the way her mouth looked plump and delicious and well kissed.

The sound of muffled laughter reached him, and his gaze shifted toward the door. Two couples walked by, each arm in arm. Probably going to the movie theater two blocks down. Their presence reminded him that a lot of people walked by the glass storefront. A private spot this definitely was not. And privacy was definitely going to be necessary.

Walking back to Mallory, he lightly clasped her hands. "You okay?"

"Yes." A wry grin curved her lips. "Just suffering from a bad case of *kissus interruptus.*"

He couldn't help but laugh. "Me, too. Still, we were most likely literally saved by the bell. If that kiss had continued…" He raised their joined hands to his lips and pressed a kiss to her fingers. "Well, given our gold-fish-bowl location, better that the kiss was interrupted by the phone than having what would have happened next interrupted by an arresting officer."

He released her hands then drew her closer. When their bodies touched from chest to knee, when the hard ridge of his erection pressed between them, he said, "Still harboring any doubts that you're incredibly sexy?"

"I'm definitely feeling less troll-like."

"Good—but still in need of further reassurance— I hope."

"A girl can never get too much reassurance."

"I can't understand how you could ever see yourself as anything other than beautiful and desirable."

Her blush deepened. "Thank you."

"You're welcome. You want me to punch what's-his-name?"

Her lips twitched. "Would you?"

"Gladly."

"What if I told you he was six foot five and weighed two-forty?"

"I'd say that would make things more difficult, but at the end of the day, I'd make damn sure he looked worse and hurt worse than me."

"As much as I appreciate the offer, he isn't worth the time or effort."

"All right. But the offer stands." Leaning forward, he touched his lips to the soft bit of fragrant skin just below her ear. "You, on the other hand," he whispered against her neck, "are very much worth my time and effort. As I recall, I promised to treat you to another bacon cheeseburger if things didn't work out with what's-his-name. Since two of those artery-cloggers in one day would probably land us in the hospital, could I interest you in dinner somewhere a little nicer than the diner?"

"Actually, I came here to invite *you* to dinner. As I recall you like seafood and I make a mean pasta with shrimp."

"You're offering to cook for me?"

"I am. Interested?"

"Absolutely." He straightened and looked into her eyes. Just to make sure there was no misunderstanding of his intentions, he laid his cards on the table. "But in a hell of a lot more than just pasta. Interested?"

Her eyes darkened and she didn't hesitate. "Absolutely."

That single word sizzled a bolt of wild lust through him. "When did you have in mind?"

"Why not tonight? Or do you have other plans?"

He smiled. "It seems I do—with a beautiful woman and a bowl of pasta and shrimp."

A layer of the shadows lurking in her eyes vanished

and she smiled. "Great." Her gaze cut to the stack of papers on the desk where he'd been working when she'd arrived. "Do you have things you still need to finish up here?"

"A few. Shouldn't take me much more than an hour."

"Actually that's perfect since I need to stop at the supermarket." She glanced at her watch. "It's six-thirty now. Why don't we say around eight o'clock, and if you can get there earlier, fine."

"Sounds great. I'll bring the wine." He released her, reluctantly, but consoled himself with the fact that they had the entire night ahead of them.

She slipped a card from her purse and handed it to him. "Here's my address. It's only about six miles from here." She gave him directions, then added, "My cell and home numbers are listed on the card. Call if you get lost."

"Not to worry, Mallory. Believe me, I'll find you."

6

Saturday, 8:00 p.m.

WHEN MALLORY HEARD A CAR pull into the driveway, her heart beat so hard she could feel the pulsing in her stomach. Hear it in her ears. Good grief, she was reacting like a teenager going on her first date.

She blinked. Actually, this was exactly the way she'd felt as a teenager when she'd gone on her first date with Adam. They'd gone to the movies. The latest James Bond flick. And hadn't watched a minute of the film. The instant the lights went down, the mother of all make-out sessions had started. To this day she blushed any time that particular film was mentioned.

Her common sense firmly told both her heart and hormones that this evening with Adam was nothing more than a bandage for her scraped-up ego and that to think of it as anything more would be foolish and fall into the category of "rebounditis." Certainly it wasn't smart to get involved with another man literally within minutes after breaking up with the last guy. Especially a guy like Adam, whose life and future were so up in the air and who was heading to Europe for three months in less than forty-eight hours. Him coming over was simply about healing her battered self-esteem and reinflating her squashed ego.

It wasn't as if she were embarking on another *relationship*. Heck, no. Nothing beyond this dinner would happen between her and Adam. Nothing deeper than a night of no-strings sex. A one-night stand with a stranger had never been her style, but Adam was certainly no stranger. And the way he'd reacted to her, looked at her with that same naked raw heat that had always lit her on fire, was exactly what she needed to pick herself up, dust herself off and restore her feminine confidence.

That kiss they'd shared at Picture This had imbued her with the same wild abandon he'd inspired in her years ago. A feeling she hadn't ever quite recaptured since. Yet the thought of being with him again, however briefly, brought all those delicious feelings screaming back. She'd be a fool not to revel in them while she had the chance.

Hearing the car door slam, she took a quick mental and visual inventory to make sure everything was as she wanted it. Norah Jones's latest ballad floated from the living-room speakers where the stereo was tuned to her favorite evening radio program, *Sensuous Songs and Decadent Dedications*. Lamps strategically lit to cast the rooms with soft light. Salad, peeled shrimp and a tray of antipasto in the fridge, loaf of French bread ready to pop in the oven, skillet and pasta pot set on the stove. Her best crystal wine goblets on the snack bar next to a grouping of cream-colored pillar candles waiting to be lit. Air conditioner unit humming in the den—and her bedroom. Where she'd stashed a trio of condoms in her bedside table.

Romantic music, food, candles, condoms—yup, she was ready for anything.

The doorbell rang and her heart jangled in response. She drew a calming breath, then smoothed her nervous hands over her silvery gray satin tank top and full turquoise skirt that skimmed a few inches above her knees. Walking to the door, she discovered her legs weren't quite steady and she suddenly wished she'd worn flats instead of her high-heeled strappy silver sandals. *Too late now.* After sucking in a final calming breath, she opened the door. And all sense of calm instantly evaporated.

In spite of the fact that she'd known Adam would be standing there, the sight of him, at her home, looking good enough to eat, sizzled a bolt of heat and lust right down her unsteady legs to her toes. Like it wasn't already hot enough, here he was, causing his own Adam-induced heat wave. And by just *standing there.*

In one hand he held a brown shopping bag bearing the local liquor store's logo. In the other hand he held a single lavender rose, an offering that tightened her throat. Their last night together that long-ago summer, the night before she'd left for college, he'd brought her a single rose. A yellow one. Told her it stood for friendship. Then told her he thought they were too young to be so involved. That they should cool things off, see other people. She couldn't help but wonder what lavender stood for.

As if nature needed to get in on the act of announcing his arrival, a flash of lightning lit the distant sky, followed by a low rumble of thunder.

"Hi," he said with a smile.

Good thing he'd said something, otherwise she most likely would have just stood there and gawked. "Hi." She opened the door wider and stepped back. "C'mon in."

After he entered, she closed and locked the door then turned to face him. Since her knees weren't as solid as she'd have liked, she leaned her shoulders against the door for support.

He set the shopping bag on the hardwood floor and slowly twirled the rose between his fingers—a mesmerizing motion—but not nearly as hypnotic as the unmistakable heat and admiration in his eyes.

"For you," he said, holding out the flower.

Mallory took the bud, noting her hands suffered from the same less-than-steady affliction as her knees. Closing her eyes, she buried her nose in the velvety petals and breathed in the heady scent. Then she looked at him and smiled.

"Thank you. It's beautiful. I've never seen a rose this color before."

"The florist said it's called 'silver lilac.' It reminded me of you."

"Oh? How's that?"

He stepped forward, until less than two feet separated them. Reaching out, he snagged her hand that held the rose, then guided the flower slowly along her jaw.

"It's soft," he said, raising his other hand to skim a single fingertip over her collarbone. "Just like you. And beautiful. Just like you."

Leaning down, he touched his lips to the spot where her neck and shoulder met, then breathed in. Tingles of pleasure vibrated along her skin and she was grateful for the solid door behind her.

"It smells incredible," he whispered, his warm breath against her skin initiating another round of tingles. "Just like you." He straightened and looked at her through serious dark blue eyes. "The florist said the color stands for rarity. Which describes you perfectly. It's unique. Rare. Different. Extraordinary. Just like you."

Whew. She needed to turn up the AC because it felt like her pores were emitting steam. And she needed a dictionary. Stat. 'Cause it appeared she'd forgotten how to speak English. The fact that his gaze was roaming over her in a way that suggested he'd like to melt off her clothing with his eyes—and hey, wouldn't that be a handy talent—did nothing to help her regain her ability to speak.

"You look gorgeous," he said softly. Moving her hand lower, he brushed the rose over her breasts. Her nipples tightened at the mere whisper of a touch and her breath caught in her throat. "I like this shirt. This material. A lot. I see you in it and all I can think is, 'Wow—she comes with her own satin sheets.'"

Releasing her hand, he reached out and planted his palms on the door next to her shoulders, bracketing her in. The warm, clean scent of him filled her head, and even though he wasn't touching her, she felt his heat, his strength, surrounding her. Enveloping her in a sensual haze. No doubt about it—she'd gone to the right guy to make her feel desirable and attractive. But then, everything about him—the way he'd touched her, looked at her—had always made her feel so much a woman.

Before she could even exhale a sigh of pleasure at being imprisoned in such a delightful way, he leaned in and kissed her.

Her heart rate tripled the instant his lips touched hers. He kept the contact light, teasing her with feathery kisses and light nibbles. On her lips. Across her jaw. Down her neck. Not touching her with anything other than his mouth. God help her, she couldn't recall ever being so utterly aroused—and he hadn't even touched her.

He dipped his tongue into the sensitive hollow at the base of her throat, the spot where she knew he would feel her rapid, erratic pulse. Her eyes drifted closed and the back of her head thunked lightly against the door. Quivers raced through her as he kissed his way up the side of her neck until his teeth lightly grazed her earlobe.

Want rocketed through her, igniting a demand for more that shook her with its intensity. She couldn't recall the last time she'd wanted a man's hands on her this badly. This desperately. It flashed through her mind that the last time had been with this man, but stark need was melting her ability to think clearly. With a moan, she blindly tossed her rose toward the small rectangular oak table in the entryway where she deposited her keys and mail and hoped the flower landed safely. Then she ran her hands up Adam's chest, over his shoulders, and buried her fingers in his thick hair. Raising up on her toes, she dragged his mouth to hers and pressed herself against him.

He groaned—although in all fairness, that ragged sound might have come from her—and in the blink of an eye he was touching her with a hell of a lot more than just his mouth. His arms went around her, one large hand sliding up into her hair and cupping her head while his other hand skimmed down her spine to settle, fingers splayed, on the small of her back. Her body, her senses, recognized him. His taste. His scent. The strong, solid feel of him pressed against her from chest to knee. The hard ridge of his erection pressing low and insistent against her belly. The delicious friction of his tongue mating intimately with hers. Saturated in sensation, their kiss sparked an almost excruciating desperation to claw off his clothes so he could put out this damn fire he'd started.

Skin…she wanted to feel his skin. She jerked his shirt from the waistband of his jeans, then plunged her hands beneath the soft material to run her palms up his smooth back. Warm. He was so warm. And solid. And he felt so good. And she wanted more.

Grabbing the ends of his shirt, she tugged upward. "Off," she demanded in a ragged whisper against his lips. "Off *now*."

He helped and seconds later his shirt landed on the floor, leaving nothing to impede her impatient hands from roaming over his lovely flesh. He was broader, more muscular, more well defined than he'd been nine years ago. Her avid gaze and eager fingers ran over him, tracing the whorls of dark hair that spread across his chest then funneled down into a silky strand that bisected his ridged abdomen before disappearing into the waistband of his jeans.

He weakened her knees further with another one of those deep, lush kisses while his fingers slipped under the thin straps of her satin tank top and lowered them down her arms, tugging gently downward until her aching breasts were free.

He cupped her flesh, his fingers teasing her nipples, dragging a low moan from her throat. His lips left hers to trail a hot path down her throat, then lower until she felt his tongue circling her nipple. Pleasure shuddered through her and she rifled her fingers through his dark hair, watching him lave her hard nipple, then draw the tight bud into the delicious heat of his mouth. Each erotic pull of his lips set up an answering pull deep in her womb and she arched her back in a silent plea for more.

Her choppy breathing hitched when his hands coasted over her hips, down her thighs, then under her full skirt. His fingers glided slowly up her bare legs and slid beneath the wisp of sheer lace of her panties. In a heartbeat he'd slid her panties down her legs and helped her step out of them.

When he straightened, their gazes collided for a brief instant and the heat burning in his eyes singed her. Then he was kissing her again, hooking a hand beneath her knee to raise it. She immediately wrapped her calf around his hip. And all bets were off.

He assaulted her senses on all fronts—his lips and tongue dancing with hers, one long-fingered hand teasing her breasts, and the other talented hand gliding along the back of her bare raised thigh to lightly knead her bottom, then play with her aching sex.

At the first glide of his fingers over her wet, swollen folds, she groaned…a deep rumbling vibration that turned into a purr of pleasure. He teased her mercilessly, and with such unerring accuracy in finding the exact rhythm her body craved, it was as if only hours instead of years had passed since he'd made love to her. As if he recalled precisely what she liked. How she loved being touched right…oooooh…there. Just like… aaaaah…that.

She felt him slip one, then two fingers inside her, stroking, caressing her, driving her relentlessly closer to the edge. Breaking off their kiss, she gulped in air, her head dropping limply back to roll against the door. He immediately feasted on her exposed neck, kissing, nipping, licking, while his fingers drove her wild. *Just one more, one more stroke…*

Her orgasm slammed into her, pulsing through her with tremors that ripped a cry from her throat…a cry that dissolved into a long pleasure-filled moan as the spasms slowly tapered off.

Breathless, boneless, heart pounding, she opened her eyes. Adam was looking at her, his expression stark with arousal, his own breathing labored. He'd wrapped his arms around her, thank goodness as they were the only thing keeping her upright.

"Whoa," she managed to say. "You need to come

with a warning label: Caution—Loss of All Control Directly Ahead." No real surprise—that was exactly how he'd affected her in the past. Still, she'd thought she would have outgrown that reaction to him.

Apparently not.

"In that case, you need a warning label, too. Caution— This Woman Will Make You Forget Time, Place and Your Own Damn Name—Just by Looking at You. But that's no shocker since that's the way it always was with you."

Surprise crept through her postorgasmic haze at his words. For her, their lovemaking, the way he'd made her feel, had been nothing short of miraculous, and in her naïveté she'd just assumed it was the same for him as he'd always seemed satisfied. But when he'd suggested they take a break, see other people, she'd concluded that he obviously hadn't been so satisfied after all.

His hands dropped to lightly knead her bottom through the material of her skirt, effectively dissolving every thought from her head. "Believe it or not," he said in a husky voice, "it wasn't my intention to pounce on you the minute I walked in the door."

"Oh? Bummer."

He leaned in and chuckled against her neck, the vibration curling spirals of warmth down to her toes. "I like to think I've acquired a little more finesse than that, but, well, I find you…" He straightened and looked into her eyes. "Irresistible."

Mallory looped her arms around his neck and rubbed her pelvis slowly against the hard bulge in his jeans. "Not to put too fine a point on it, but I think I'm the one who pounced on you."

"Uh-huh. And how many complaints did you hear?"

"None. But I'm the one who reaped all the benefits."

His clever fingers walked her skirt up and his hands curved over her bare butt, lifting her higher against him. "I wouldn't say that. Besides, the night's still young."

"Hmm. Already I can see what will be my biggest weakness in any dealings with you."

"What's that?"

"My knees."

"Ah. Which would mean a lot of lying down. A terrible problem, but I'm all kinds of empathetic."

"Lying down…now that sounds like a great idea." Reaching around, she slid her hands over his and gently slipped from his grasp. Entwining their fingers, she was about to lead him toward her bedroom when the lights suddenly flickered. She paused and they flickered madly again, then went out, plunging the room into darkness.

7

"HEY, WHO TURNED OUT THE lights?" Adam asked, mourning the fact that the best view in all of New York had disappeared from right in front of him in the blink of an eye. He moved to stand directly behind Mallory, his chest pressed to her back. Settling his hands against her smooth stomach, he lightly brushed his thumbs along the soft undersides of her breasts. "Did you forget to pay your electric bill?"

She leaned back against him, raising her arms up and back to encircle his neck. "Nope. Power must have gone out. It'll probably come back on in a minute. Mmm…" Her voice trailed off as his fingers lightly teased her nipples.

"In the meanwhile, I've got you all to myself in the dark."

"So it would seem." She wriggled her bottom against his straining erection and a low growl rumbled in his throat.

"If you keep doing that, we won't make it to the bedroom," he warned, nuzzling her soft nape. A delicate shiver ran through her and he inwardly smiled. Ah, yes, she still liked that particular spot. And she was still as incredibly responsive. Uninhibited. Fascinating. Exciting. But then, everything about her had fascinated and captivated him, in and out of bed. Her laughter. Her spirit. Her kind, generous nature. Based on all the magic she'd made him feel, there was no need to question why so many songs and poems were devoted to the wonder of first love.

"We might not make it from this very spot." She turned in his arms, one hand skimming into his hair to urge his mouth to hers while her other hand glided down to stroke him through his jeans. "I don't suppose you have a condom handy?" she asked in a breathless whisper against his lips.

He instantly cursed the fact that he hadn't slipped one into his back pocket. "In the bag I brought." Which meant his supply was less than ten feet away—which at the moment seemed like ten miles.

Her fingers slipped beneath his waistband and brushed over the head of his penis through his boxer briefs. Heat shot through him and he sucked in a hissing breath.

"Hmm. You brought wine, a rose *and* condoms," she murmured in a smoky voice. "Good combination."

Trailing his hands up and down her bare back, he said, "I thought so. But I'm thinking maybe I didn't bring enough condoms."

"Oh? How many did you bring?"

"Only a dozen."

She chuckled and grazed her fingertips over him

again, dulling his vision. "That should last us till dinner. After that we can dip into my supply. Of course, if the power doesn't come on soon, cooking isn't going to happen."

"No problem. I'm happy with the cooking that's going on right here. Kitchen—not necessary." He slid his hands beneath her skirt, loving the way her breath caught at the gesture. "It's not what you have for dinner, it's who you have it with."

"Glad you think so, although I had planned to impress you with my pasta."

"Sweetheart, you've already impressed me. I'd be happy with peanut butter. Believe me, the way to a man's heart isn't through his stomach—it's farther south."

"I see." With a flick of her fingers, she opened the button on his jeans, and a breath of relief escaped him. "You're going to get hungry eventually, Adam."

"I'm hungry right now." He leaned down and lightly bit the side of her neck. "Starving, in fact."

She slowly lowered his zipper, and he went still in an agony of anticipation for her touch.

"So…do you prefer the bedroom, or the sofa?" she asked. Her fingers wrapped around his erection and lightly squeezed, derailing his entire train of thought. After several seconds of stroking him, she made a *tsking* sound then said, "You seem to be having difficulty making a decision."

He said the only word he could manage. "Huh?"

His eyes had grown accustomed to the darkness and he saw the sexy smile that curved her lips while she continued her driving-him-insane caress. "Bedroom or sofa?"

For an answer, he swung her up into his arms and carried her toward the den's long sectional sofa as it was closer—only a room's length away.

"My choice is you," he muttered, nipping kisses along her jaw as he crossed the room. "On the sofa. In the bed. I don't care. As long as it's you. Now."

"Now sounds good to me."

He deposited her on the plush cushion where she landed with a gentle bounce. Even in the dim light, there was no mistaking the arousal glittering in her eyes. His gaze skimmed over her, taking in her lush mouth, her full breasts topped with aroused nipples and her hiked-up skirt that revealed the triangle of dark curls at the apex of her thighs. His temperature jumped up a few more degrees and he clenched his hands to keep from reaching for her. Much as he hated to leave her for even an instant, he knew he'd better get a condom now. Once he touched her again, all bets would be off.

He quickly strode back to the shopping bag in the foyer and rummaged through the assortment of things he'd purchased. He'd just snatched up the box of condoms when a sharp knock sounded at the door.

For several seconds he remained still, breathing hard, then his gaze jumped to Mallory, who looked startled. Before either of them could say anything, or even move, another series of sharp knocks sounded.

"Mallory?" came a muffled female voice accompanied by more insistent knocking. "Are you there, dear?

It's me, Mrs. Trigali. Helllllooooo. Are you there? Oh, I hope you are. Please answer the door."

Based on the way Mallory jumped to her feet and struggled to pull up her top, Adam suspected that he unfortunately wasn't going to be needing a condom quite as soon as he'd thought.

His suspicions were confirmed when she called out, "I'm here, Mrs. Trigali. Just give me a minute."

Still adjusting her straps, she hurried over to him, and said, "I'm so sorry… If it were anyone else, I'd ignore it." She reached down and scooped up her panties and his shirt. "But she's my next-door neighbor and she lives alone and she sounds worried."

He dropped the box of condoms back into the shopping bag, torn between the desire to yank out his hair in frustration and an inexplicable urge to laugh. Jeez, some things never changed. Clearly the timing curse that had plagued them in the past was still alive and well in the present.

"No problem." Wincing, he zipped up—very carefully— then took his Polo shirt from her. He slipped the soft cotton over his head, leaving it untucked. "But I'm gonna want a rain check."

"Me, too."

"All right, two rain checks."

She laughed, and stepped into her panties. "I meant I'm going to want a rain check *also*."

"Heeelllooo," came Mrs. Trigali's muffled voice, accompanied by more knocking. "Mallory?"

"Coming," she called out. Then she stood on her toes and brushed a quick kiss against his mouth. "I really am sorry. I owe you one."

"A second ago you said *two*."

"Okay, two."

"How about three?"

"I'll think about it. Why don't you go in the den and have a seat?"

"'Fraid sitting wouldn't be comfortable yet. You want me to make myself scarce?"

"Only if you want to," she said, heading toward the door. "But if you stay there, brace yourself for a barrage of questions."

Before he could reply, she pulled open the door. The beam of a powerful flashlight arced into the foyer and he raised a hand to protect his eyes.

"*There* you are, my dear," said Mrs. Trigali, crossing the threshold, her flashlight beam bouncing around before finally settling on Mallory.

"Are you all right, Mrs. Trigali?" Mallory asked.

"Oh, yes, I'm fine. I was just worried when you didn't answer right away that you'd started the meeting without me."

"Meeting?"

"Why, the block captains' meeting. Surely under such circumstances we'll be having one."

"Circumstances?"

"Why, the blackout, of course."

She stepped farther into the foyer and her flashlight beam fell on Adam. "Ah, I see I'm not the first to arrive."

First to arrive? Adam thought. Oh boy, that didn't sound good.

Mrs. Trigali moved closer to him, peering over the

edge of gold-rimmed bifocals. "You must be new to the neighborhood."

"Actually, I don't live in the neighborhood. I'm a friend of Mallory's." Adam extended his hand. "Adam Clayton."

Mrs. Trigali narrowed her eyes and gave him an assessing look his grandma Amy would have called "the once-over twice." His lips twitched as he realized that this petite woman dressed in a crisp sleeveless blouse, khaki shorts that reached her knees and canvas sneakers reminded him of his grandmother. Her short, snow-white hair was cut in the same no-nonsense style, and she pursed her lips the same way as Grandma Amy. He figured he must have passed muster because after her scrutiny, she nodded then shook his hand. "Sophia Trigali."

"Pleased to meet you, ma'am."

"What's this about a blackout?" Mallory asked.

Mrs. Trigali's eyebrows shot up and her gaze bounced between her and Adam. "Didn't notice that the lights went out, huh?"

Mallory felt a heated blush creep all the way up to her hairline and was grateful that the foyer wasn't illuminated by anything brighter than Mrs. Trigali's flashlight. Her gaze flicked to Adam, but he looked supremely calm and even a bit amused at her neighbor's not-so-subtle question.

"We noticed," Mallory said, "but figured it was just a momentary power failure."

"Nothing momentary about it," Mrs. Trigali reported. "Will you hold this for me, young man?" she asked Adam, handing him her flashlight.

"Sure." He guided the light as Mrs. Trigali slid a canvas tote from her shoulder, setting the bag on the floor. Then she pulled a black object the size of a hardback book from the bag.

"My emergency radio," Mrs. Trigali said, turning one of the dials. "It runs on batteries. Always Be Prepared, that's my motto."

"Actually, I think that's the Boy Scout motto," Mallory said with a grin.

"And smart young men those Scouts are."

She made an adjustment to a knob and an announcer's voice boomed, "... have confirmed that the power outage, which affects all of New York state, New Jersey and parts of Connecticut, is the result of a system failure. The exact cause of the failure is not known at this time, but authorities do not believe that foul play was involved. Officials and technicians are working to restore power, but have not yet announced any estimates as to when the system will go back on line. This station intends to return to our regular broadcast schedule, with frequent updates between dedications to keep you apprised of all the latest developments. Again, authorities believe that—"

Mrs. Trigali muted the volume and shook her head. "System failure. You can bet *that's* not going to be fixed in the next few hours. That's why I figured we'd be having an emergency block captains' meeting." She nodded toward her bag. "I brought my emergency kit— citronella candles, waterproof matches, three more flashlights, extra batteries, a box of crackers, some ham and provolone, a jar of olives, a loaf of semolina from

Luigi's bakery, a bottle of Chianti and some cards in case anybody's up for a little canasta." She shot Adam a piercing look. "You know how to play canasta, young man?"

Mallory watched Adam's lips twitch with obvious amusement, and a feeling of gratitude washed through her for his patience with both the ill-timed interruption and her talkative neighbor. She knew damn well certain men—like Greg—wouldn't have been such good sports under the circumstances. But his kindness and patience had attracted her from the day she'd met him.

"Yes, ma'am, I know how to play canasta."

"Humph. You any good?"

He smiled. "My grandma Amy taught me everything she knows—and now she has a hard time beating me."

Mrs. Trigali's expression turned fierce. "You mean to tell me you don't let your poor granny win?"

Adam laughed. "If Grandma Amy even suspected that I'd purposely tossed a game, she'd whack me upside my head with her purse—and that purse of hers could cause a concussion."

"Sounds like my kind of gal," Mrs. Trigali said with a grin. "We're looking for a fourth for our Thursday afternoon game. She live around here?"

Adam shook his head. "South Carolina."

She heaved a mournful sigh. "Drat. You don't live in South Carolina, do you?"

"No. Manhattan."

"Your grandma coming up to visit you any time soon?"

"In November. For her birthday. She's turning seventy-five, but last time I saw her, she informed me that seventy-five is the new sixty. Based on how active she is, I believe it."

Mallory was about to interrupt, suspecting by the speculative look in Mrs. Trigali's eyes that Adam was about to be bombarded with a barrage of personal questions of the "are you married, what do you do for a living, how are your finances" variety, but before she could say a word, a loud knocking sounded on the door.

"Anybody home?" came a muffled masculine voice. "Don't start the meeting without me."

"Oh, it's that pest Ray Finney," Mrs. Trigali said in an undertone, her features pinching with clear displeasure. "I should have known he'd show up. Well, if he thinks he's getting any of my ham and provolone, he's mistaken."

Mallory pressed her lips together to hide her amusement and headed toward the door. From the first day Mr. Finney had moved into the small ranch next door to Mrs. Trigali three months ago, they'd rubbed each other the wrong way. She complained that he made too much noise with his power tools, and he thought she was a busybody.

When she opened the door, she was greeted by a heat-wave induced blast of hot, humid air and Mr. Finney who carried a flashlight in one hand and a large canvas tote similar to Mrs. Trigali's in the other. As always, his full head of white hair was neatly combed and his tortoise-shell-rimmed bifocals rode low on his nose. He wore his usual summer attire of rumpled, short-sleeved tropical-print shirt, wrinkled khaki shorts and battered deck shoes.

"The meeting hasn't started yet, has it?" he asked with a smile, stepping into the foyer.

Before Mallory could answer, he caught sight of Mrs. Trigali and he froze, his smile faltering. He jerked his head in a nod. "Evening, Sophia."

Mrs. Trigali raised her chin. "Ray."

Mallory introduced Adam and the two men shook hands.

"What do you have in that tote bag, Ray?" Mrs. Trigali asked, eyeing the canvas bag as if it contained snakes.

"My emergency supplies." He ticked off items on his fingers. "Battery-operated radio, extra flashlights and batteries, candles, matches, a bottle of single-malt scotch, a deck of cards and poker chips, Oreo cookies and canned spaghetti with meatballs—and a can opener."

"*Canned* spaghetti and meatballs?" Mrs. Trigali said, her nose wrinkling with obvious distaste. "What sort of man eats *canned* spaghetti and meatballs?"

"The sort of man who doesn't know how to cook something unless he can slap it on a grill." He turned his attention to Mallory. "Carl and Tina Webber are out of town, so they won't be coming to the meeting. I'm not sure about Wanda Newton."

"Wanda's in Jersey this weekend visiting her son," Mrs. Trigali said. "So it's just us," she and Mr. Finney said in unison. They turned and glared at each other.

Wanting to forestall an argument and get her evening with Adam back on track, Mallory quickly interjected, "Mrs. Trigali, I keep my emergency supplies in the kitchen. Do you think you could bring your flashlight to help me find them?"

"Of course, my dear." She directed her beam of light toward the archway that led to Mallory's kitchen and moved forward.

"We'll be right back," Mallory murmured, shooting Adam a quick smile. To her relief, his good humor was clearly still intact as he smiled in return and shot her a wink. To her further relief, there was no missing the desire banked in his eyes.

As soon as she entered the kitchen, Mrs. Trigali grabbed her hand and pulled her to the farthest corner. The low murmur of male voices reached them, indicating Adam and Mr. Finney were chatting.

"Okay, tell me everything," Mrs. Trigali whispered.

"Everything about what?" Mallory whispered back.

Mrs. Trigali looked toward the ceiling. "About your new young man. You can start by telling me what happened to your other man, Greg."

"We're no longer together."

Mrs. Trigali nodded, her sharp eyes alight with… something. "Aha. I *knew* something wasn't right there."

"You did?"

"Of course. You dated him for months, yet you still weren't in love with him. If you haven't fallen in love after all that time, it's never going to happen."

Well, hell. *Now* she gets this great advice. "Why didn't you tell me this before?" Mallory asked, half-joking.

"You didn't ask me. Besides, that's the sort of thing

a woman has to find out for herself. Now tell me, when and where did you meet this Adam?"

Mallory suppressed a knowing grin. She'd known the questions would come and it occurred to her as it often did that her neighbor would make a fine newspaper reporter. She had a nose for a story and an uncanny knack for ferreting out information. Some people, namely Mr. Finney, found that trait annoying, but Mallory found Mrs. Trigali's ways endearing and motherly. Her husband had passed away five years ago after forty years of marriage, and Mallory knew the woman suffered from bouts of loneliness. At least once a month they had dinner together to swap stories and recipes.

"Adam and I have known each other for years, even dated briefly, but we lost touch about five years ago. We bumped into each other last week and—"

"And here he is. So he's 'The One Who Got Away.'" Mrs. Trigali's dark eyes lit up with unmistakable excitement. "I just read an article about this in *Metro Chick* magazine. Did you know that eighty-eight percent of women who meet up again with 'The One Who Got Away' discover that he's 'The One'? *Eighty-eight percent,* my dear."

Mallory couldn't help but chuckle. "So I've recently heard. When did you start reading *Metro Chick?*"

"Just started. My fifteen-year-old granddaughter bought me a subscription saying I needed to 'get more hip' and 'check out the hotties.' I must say, after just one issue, I've learned a lot. Who knew lip gloss came in so many flavors? And did you know that two out of three men prefer the cherry-flavored?"

"To wear?" Mallory teased.

"No, my dear. To *kiss*. I drove right over to Walgreens and bought some."

"Oh? Who are you planning to kiss?"

Mrs. Trigali became visibly flustered. "No one. But you know my motto—Always Be Prepared. But back to your new young man—now *he's* what *Metro Chick* would call a hottie. Wanna borrow my lip gloss?"

Smothering a laugh, Mallory reached out and hugged the woman. "That's very sweet, but I already have some."

"Good. Make sure you use it. I like your Adam. He's a fine young man, I can tell. He's polite and he clearly loves his grandma. That counts for a lot."

"We're only friends."

"Perhaps for now—but don't forget. *Eighty-eight* percent."

"We have...very different lives. I'm not planning that we'll even see each other after tonight." She firmly ignored the unsettling flutter her words caused in her midsection.

Mrs. Trigali studied her over the rims of her bifocals for several long seconds, then said, "That may be *your* plan, my dear, but I don't believe it's his."

"What do you mean?"

"I saw how he looked at you." She leaned closer and her voice dropped even lower. "He's *very* interested."

Yes—very interested in picking up where they'd left off. As was she. But there was nothing more to it than that. Of course, she wasn't about to share tidbits *that* personal with Mrs. Trigali.

"He's leaving for an extended trip to Europe the day after tomorrow, and after that he's off to God knows where for who knows how long. Then there's a good chance he may move away from New York. We're only getting together this evening," Mallory repeated as firmly as a whisper would allow. "And that's it."

Mrs. Trigali's jaw sawed back and forth several times, the way it did when the wheels in her mind were furiously turning. Finally she nodded decisively and said, "Well, if you only have tonight, then you certainly can't waste your time with a block captains' meeting. As soon as we've gathered your emergency supplies, I'll hustle that pest Ray Finney out of here so you and your young man can enjoy your one evening together. I'll leave you my ham, provolone and Chianti." She shook her finger. "Mark my words—the way to a man's heart is through his stomach."

Mallory pressed her lips together to hold in the laughter that threatened to escape. No way was she going to tell Mrs. Trigali what Adam had said about that particular theory. "Thanks, but I have plenty of food and wine here," she said.

"What kind of food? Not canned spaghetti, I hope." A visible shudder ran through Mrs. Trigali.

"Nothing canned," Mallory promised with a smile. "I made antipasto."

"Ah. Excellent choice. It's hearty *and* offers a selection of things to nibble on. According to *Metro Chick,* men like that."

"I'll keep that in mind."

They spent the next few minutes locating candles, a

half-dozen of which Mallory lit, along with her pillar candles, casting the kitchen in a cozy, golden glow that spilled out into the breakfast room and foyer. After putting fresh batteries in two flashlights, she and Mrs. Trigali headed back to the foyer where Adam and Mr. Finney were deep in conversation.

"Now that I'm retired, I have the time to indulge my hobbies," Mr. Finney was saying. "Be happy to show you the shop I've set up in my garage any time you'd like to stop by."

"Thanks," said Adam with a smile. "I've always had a weakness for power tools."

"Typical man," Mallory teased, handing him one of her flashlights. "Likes anything that goes 'vrrroooom.'"

Their fingers brushed when his curled around the light's handle and a barrage of tingles jittered up her arm. Ridiculous. Or maybe it was more the way he was looking at her that caused the tingles.

"Not just any power tools," he said. "Mr. Finney has a top-of-the-line, model XJ586 power saw."

Mrs. Trigali fixed a laserlike glare on Mr. Finney. "Is that the thing you use in your garage that makes all that racket?"

"It makes some noise," Mr. Finney said calmly, "but it's music to my ears."

"Then you must be tone-deaf," Mrs. Trigali said with a sniff.

"Can't cut the wood to make furniture without making a little noise," he countered.

"A *little* noise would be fine. And a huge improvement. But we can argue about it later. Let's go."

"I don't want to argue with you, Sophia—" Mr. Finney's brows snapped down. "Go?"

"The meeting's been canceled."

"What do you mean, canceled? There are issues that need to be discussed—"

"Fine," Mrs. Trigali broke in, picking up her belongings. "It's not canceled. But it's being relocated. To my house." She set her radio on the small table near the door. "I'll leave this with you so you can keep up with the blackout news."

"But what about you?" Mallory asked.

"I have another one at home." She flicked a glance at Ray. "Let's go." She headed toward the door, her flashlight beam dancing in front of her.

Mr. Finney's confused gaze shifted from Mrs. Trigali to Adam to the radio to Mallory. "You're not coming to the meeting?" he asked Mallory.

"No, she's not," Mrs. Trigali said in a tart voice from the door.

"But why…?" Mr. Finney's voice trailed off as his gaze again bounced from Mallory to Adam. Understanding dawned in his eyes, followed by a flicker of amusement. "I see."

"About time," Mrs. Trigali stated. "Since I'm not getting any younger, let's get this show on the road. I don't suppose you know how to play canasta?"

Mr. Finney turned and stared at her. "I don't suppose you know how to play poker?"

Mrs. Trigali muttered something under her breath in Italian. Mallory wasn't sure what the translation was, but based on the woman's expression it wasn't complimentary. They all walked to the door where Adam shook hands with both Mr. Finney and Mrs. Trigali and Mallory gave them quick hugs.

"Be careful," she called from the open doorway, watching them make their way down the short cement path leading to the sidewalk. Mr. Finney gallantly took Mrs. Trigali's arm.

"I can walk by myself, you old coot," Mrs. Trigali said, but Mallory noted with amusement that she didn't pull her arm away. Chuckling softly, she closed and locked the door. When she turned around, she discovered Adam stood directly in front of her, highlighted by the pale golden glow spilling from the kitchen where the candles she'd lit burned.

Before she could so much as draw a breath, he dipped his knees and scooped her up into his arms.

"Now..." he murmured against her lips. "Where were we?"

8

ADAM HELD MALLORY in his arms and headed swiftly toward the darkened hallway, which he assumed led to the bedrooms. "Where's your room?" he asked.

"This way," she said, clicking on her flashlight and pointing with the beam. "Last door on the right." She nibbled on the side of his neck and he increased his pace. "Give up on the sofa?"

"I thought it best to get out of the foyer and as far away from the front door as possible. I survived one interruption—barely—and even liked your neighbors in spite of their bad timing, but it's not a scenario I want to repeat."

"Good thinking. You know, without the air-conditioning running, it's going to get really hot in here soon."

"As far as I'm concerned, it's really hot in here right now."

"Exactly. So probably we should get these clothes off."

"Couldn't agree more."

"How about first one to get naked wins a prize?" she suggested, slipping her fingers beneath the *V* opening at his neck to touch his chest.

"Works for me—especially since I don't see any-body being a loser in that contest."

No sooner had the words left his mouth than he heard a faint musical sound. He paused and listened for several seconds. "Did you leave that radio on?"

"No. That's my cell phone." She worried her bottom lip. "I should—"

"Don't even think about it." He started toward the bedroom again, but before he'd taken one step, another sound chimed in. He stopped again and groaned.

"What's that?" she asked.

"*My* cell phone."

She buried her face against his neck and made a noise that sounded like a muffled laugh. "We should probably answer them."

"You've *got* to be kidding. Whoever it is can wait." He didn't bother to add *I can't* since it seemed patently obvious. He started walking again.

"They'll just call back."

"That's what voice mail is for."

"It might be my mom," she said. "Worried about me with the blackout. If I don't pick up, she might decide to drive over here."

That stopped him like he'd walked into a brick wall. "Where's your phone?"

"Kitchen counter."

"Mine's in my bag in the foyer." Muttering a litany of very creative curses, he turned around and walked swiftly back down the hall. A noise that sounded suspiciously like a giggle vibrated against his neck. "You're not laughing, are you?"

"You have to admit this is sort of funny."

"I do? Maybe funny later. *Not* funny now."

"I guess we could ignore the ringing and call whoever it is back in ten minutes."

"Ten minutes? *Ten* minutes? Sweetheart, if you think you'll only be in that bedroom for ten minutes…" He shook his head and gently lowered her to her feet. "Not happening. Of course, I have to actually get you there first, a task that's turning into a Holy Grail–type quest."

He strode into the foyer, grabbed his bag then walked back to the kitchen. Settling himself in the far corner, he fished out his cell phone, noting that she'd already answered hers. He glanced at his missed-calls list, which indicated Nick had been the person phoning him. A spurt of guilt worked its way through his frustration. A blackout couldn't be an easy situation with a new baby.

Bracing his hips against the counter, he watched Mallory lean against the opposite wall. He dialed Nick's number, but received a busy signal. Then, in an attempt to forestall another interruption in case she heard about the blackout on the news, he dialed his mother's number in South Carolina. Her answering machine picked up and he left a brief message assuring her he was fine and he'd check in again tomorrow. Then he redialed Nick and this time the phone rang. Waiting for his friend to pick up, he noticed Mallory had ended her call and set her phone on the counter. She shot him a heated look

The Harlequin Reader Service® — Here's how it works:

NO POSTAGE
NECESSARY
IF MAILED
IN THE
UNITED STATES

BUSINESS REPLY MAIL
FIRST-CLASS MAIL   PERMIT NO. 717-003   BUFFALO, NY

POSTAGE WILL BE PAID BY ADDRESSEE

HARLEQUIN READER SERVICE
3010 WALDEN AVE
PO BOX 1867
BUFFALO NY 14240-9952

Do You Have the LUCKY KEY?

PLAY THE Lucky Key Game

and you can get

FREE BOOKS and a FREE GIFT!

Scratch the gold areas with a coin. Then check below to see the books and gift you can get!

YES!

I have scratched off the gold areas. Please send me the 2 FREE BOOKS and GIFT for which I qualify. I understand I am under no obligation to purchase any books, as explained on the back of this card.

351 HDL D7X3   151 HDL D7Y4

FIRST NAME	LAST NAME

ADDRESS

APT.#   CITY

STATE/ PROV.   ZIP/ POSTAL CODE

2 free books plus a free gift   1 free book

2 free books   Try Again!

www.eHarlequin.com

filled with the wickedly playful mischief he remembered so clearly—that had so thoroughly bewitched and inflamed him. Then she walked slowly toward him in a cat-stalking-its-prey way that spiked his temperature another few degrees.

Nick's voice sounded in his ear. "Hello."

With his gaze glued on Mallory, Adam said, "Hi, Nick. Everything okay?"

"Except for the no lights, no power thing, yeah, we're fine. Caroline's actually asleep, and Annie's lit a bunch of candles. I was calling to check on you. Where are you?"

All thoughts of answering were driven from his head when Mallory pressed herself against him, raised up onto her toes and lightly bit his neck.

"Hell…" he said on a soft exhalation of breath.

"Yeah, it's hot as hell. But where are you? Still at the studio?"

"No." He managed to get out the word before gritting his teeth when Mallory's hands skimmed underneath his shirt. He reached for her with his free hand, but she smiled and shook her head at him.

"Finish your call," she whispered, her fingers trailing over his abdomen. "Don't mind me."

Yeah, right.

"Damn, you're not stuck on the expressway, are you?" Nick asked. "According to the last radio news report I heard, the traffic's turning into a nightmare."

She lowered his zipper and slipped her hands inside the waistband of his boxer briefs.

"I…I'm here on the island," he managed to say. "Uh, safe and sound."

She freed his erection then slowly sank to her knees before him.

"Good. You want to come over here and crash?"

He looked down and watched her slowly swirl her tongue over the head of his penis. A guttural growl rumbled in his throat.

"Adam, dude, you okay? I can barely hear you. Damn cell phones."

"I'm...good."

She drew him into the satiny heat of her mouth, and he dropped his head back, squeezing his eyes shut. "I've gotta go, Nick."

"You coming?"

"Huh?"

"You coming over?"

"No. Thanks," he said through gritted teeth, his breathing jagged. "I've already got...ahhh...place to stay."

"Okay. Talk to you tomorrow."

"Tomorrow. Right. Bye." He shut the phone and dropped it. Before it even hit the floor, he was sifting his hands through her silky hair. Lifting his head, he watched her draw him deeper into her mouth and he sucked in a sharp breath. Every nerve ending tensed, ignited with the erotic pull of her mouth, the teasing glide of her tongue. His muscles involuntarily flexed and he thrust forward into the warm, wet heat.

Sweat broke out on his forehead and he clenched his jaw to hold off the increasing need to come. When he couldn't take any more, he grabbed her shoulders and urged her to her feet. After fastening his button to keep his pants up, he scooped her into his arms and headed purposefully toward the bedroom. She snatched up the flashlight from the counter as he walked past.

"You don't play fair," he said.

"Hey, all's fair in making love."

"Wait until it's payback time."

"Hmm. Is that a threat—or a promise?"

"Both."

"Hopefully I won't have to wait too long. But I don't know—we've headed down this hallway before."

"And *nothing* is stopping us this time. I turned off my damn phone."

She combed her fingers through his hair. "Clearly we're on the same wavelength. I did the same thing. And I spoke to my mom and best friend, reassured them of my safety, so no worries."

"Good." He entered the bedroom, then lowered her to her feet at the edge of the bed. "Now, as I recall, before we were so rudely interrupted—again—we'd just agreed we should get these clothes off."

"I remember," she said, her eyes glittering in the dim light. "Ready, set, go."

In the history of mankind, there might have been a guy who managed to get his clothes off quicker than Adam, but he strongly doubted it.

"I win," he said, eyeing her skirt and panties that she'd only managed to lower to her knees.

She released the material and they slid to the floor, pooling at her ankles, leaving her naked. Her gaze strolled slowly over him, lingering on his erection. The erotic image of her, on her knees, drawing him into her mouth, slammed into him. He could almost feel her lips gliding over him and he involuntarily jerked in response. When her gaze rose to meet his, her eyes brimmed with a heat that he imagined matched his own.

"Either you cheated, or you set some sort of world record," she said in a smoky voice.

"World record." Wanting, needing his hands on her, he reached out and clasped her hips then moved closer…until his erection brushed against her stomach. "Besides, how could I possibly cheat? Clearly I have nothing up my sleeve. Are you saying I didn't win fair and square?"

She splayed her hands on his chest then slowly rubbed herself against him. He could practically hear whatever small amount of blood still remained above his neck whooshing down from his brain to his groin.

"Actually, I was thinking that it wasn't really fair for *you* because clearly I'm going to benefit from you winning."

"That's okay. I don't mind sharing. Especially with you."

"Still, you had an unfair advantage. I'd already unzipped your jeans—"

"For which I thank you—"

"—and I had to set down the flashlight." She nodded toward the beam of light rising from the night table to point toward the ceiling, casting the bed in a hazy glow. "That cost me several crucial seconds."

"You could have just tossed it on the floor."

"True, but I was thinking of you." She raised a brow. "Still like making love with the lights on?"

"I'm flattered you remember."

"Oh, I remember plenty of things. And I can't wait to see if you still like them."

"Gotta tell ya, there's not much chance of me *not* liking anything you'd care to do."

Her gaze roamed over him while her hands ran up his chest and over his shoulders. "It's such a shame that you're not actually gorgeous," she said, heaving a dramatic sigh. "It's a real stretch for me to pretend I'm enjoying myself here, but since you're my guest…well, I suppose it must be done."

"Certainly feel free to do whatever you think must be done."

She whispered a single fingertip over the engorged head of his penis. "Clearly you're very glad to be here."

"You have no idea."

He leaned forward to kiss her, but she shook her head and stepped back. "Oh, no. You already had your wicked way with me."

"And you had yours with me in the kitchen."

"Not really. That was just to get you in the mood."

He gave a short laugh. "Like I haven't been on the verge of detonation since the minute I saw you."

"Then to *keep* you in the mood."

"Believe me, it wasn't an issue. But mission accomplished."

She stroked him again and his eyes slid closed. "So I see," she murmured. "But it's still my turn."

"Well, if you insist… Far be it from me to argue with a woman who's clearly made up her mind." Wrapping his arms around her, he lifted her against him then tumbled them onto the mattress.

"Good answer." She urged him back until he reclined with his head propped on her double row of pillows. Reaching around him, she slid open the drawer in her bedside table and withdrew a condom, which she tossed onto the bed within easy reach. Then she urged his legs apart and shifted until she knelt between his thighs.

She tickled her fingers lightly over his inner thighs. "Just lay back and relax."

"Relax?" A breath huffed from between his lips. "You can't be…" His words melted into a groan as her fingers dipped into the crease of his thighs and cupped him. "Serious," he finished.

"Oh, I'm serious. I owe you for the greeting you gave me in the foyer. And I always pay my debts."

"Good to know," he managed to say, although his ability to make small talk depleted more rapidly with every arousing pass of her hands and fingers over his flesh. "But as I recall, we agreed you owed me two. Possibly…aaahhh…three."

"Hmm, that's right. And I still owe you your prize for getting naked first on top of all that. Looks like it's going to be long night."

"That's a shame. Really—" He sucked a hissing breath as one hand wrapped around him and lightly squeezed while her other hand continued to wander lazily. His ability to string together a coherent sentence fled, so he just watched her touching him, arousing him, watched her arousal increase along with his, and let her see how profoundly she affected him.

Gritting his teeth against the intense pleasure, he endured the sweet torturous stimulation of her cupping him, stroking him, squeezing him until he was on the verge of exploding. Then he grabbed her wrists to still her marauding hands.

"Can't take any more," he said, his voice jagged with need.

He vaguely noted the gleam of feminine satisfaction in her eyes, but he was much more interested in her reach for the condom. He barely controlled the urgent need clawing at him while she rolled the protection over him. The instant she finished, she straddled him then slowly sank onto his erection.

That slow slick slide into her body ripped a groan from deep inside him and his eyes slid closed. For several seconds she remained still and he absorbed the incredible feel of her tight heat wrapped around him.

But those few seconds were all the reprieve she gave him. She rocked her hips, and he sucked in a breath. When she rocked again, he grasped her hips and thrust upward, his control rapidly deteriorating. Again and again in rhythm to her movements, harder, deeper with each stroke. A long feminine moan filled his ears and she threw her head back. The instant he felt the first ripple of her orgasm tighten around him, he let himself go. His release pounded through him, dragging a guttural sound from his throat.

She collapsed on top of him, her arms loosely encircling his head, her face pressed against his neck. Her choppy breaths puffed against his damp skin, and a memory flashed through his mind, of the two of them just like this years ago, sated, breathless, her forehead nestled on his shoulder, his hands drifting slowly up and down her bare back.

She lifted her head and their eyes met. An odd sensation enveloped his chest, sort of like his heart rolled over and stuck its little heart arms up in the air and proclaimed *Ya got me, I give up*—an unprecedented reaction for him after sex.

And usually after sex, he had no problem making light small talk. But looking into her eyes, nothing that came to mind could be categorized as "light." No, there was nothing "light" about *God, I've missed you.* Or *How the hell could I have let you get away?* Or *No one's made me feel like this since...you.*

A half smile pulled up one corner of her mouth. "Just like old times, huh?"

He mentally shook himself, but he remained unsettled by his thoughts. Echoing her half smile, he said, "I was just thinking the same thing."

"That's called 'being on the same wavelength.'"

"Yeah. Except, I was thinking that hard as it is to believe, it's even better now."

"And there's that same-wavelength thing again. Or maybe we're both just really smart."

"We are. You know, I always did like that you were smart."

She shook her head. "You did not. Not always."

"Oh, yeah? Like when?"

"Like when I'd beat your pants off at Scrabble."

"You'd beat me because I was more interested in trying to get *your* pants off than playing the game. So instead of wasting time trying to figure out a great word to fit in the triple word score, I'd flop down something like *it* or *two* or *the* just to keep the game moving along."

Even in the dim light there was no missing her incredulous expression. He had to press his lips together to keep from laughing. "Are you serious?"

"Hell, yes. What—did you think I didn't know any words with more than three letters?"

"Well, yeah. I thought you were just a really bad speller."

"Nope. Just wanted the game over with faster."

Her eyes narrowed. "I used to beat you at Monopoly, too."

"Right. 'Cause I used to make deals that were very advantageous—for you. Next thing I'd know, I was broke, you'd won the game and off came your clothes. Which, in my opinion, really made *me* the winner."

She shook her head. "Unbelievable. I can't believe you tricked me like that."

"I can't believe you'd think I'd be stupid enough to sell you half a dozen properties for a couple hundred bucks."

She lifted her chin. "Humph. Well, if you'd been *really* smart, you might have suggested an alternate way to get my clothes off sooner."

"Like what?"

"Strip Monopoly."

An image of naked real-estate wheeling and dealing popped into his mind and he grinned. "Sounds like fun. Don't suppose you have the game?"

"As a matter of fact, I do. I also have Scrabble. And

Twister. Maybe after dinner I could interest you in a little friendly competition?"

"Sweetheart, I'd be happy to play any game with you that involves stripping." An image of them, naked, assuming pretzel-like positions, flashed through his mind. "Twister sounds especially promising. Actually, I remembered how much you liked to play games, so I brought one with me."

"What game?"

"It's a surprise. For later. For now, how about I open the bottle of wine I brought?"

"Sounds great. Are you hungry yet?"

He leaned up and lightly bit her neck. "Starving."

She dropped a quick kiss on his lips then rolled off him. "Bathroom's right across the hallway," she said, handing him the flashlight. "Don't stub your toe. Or anything else. I'll meet you in the kitchen."

Five minutes later, clad in his boxer briefs, Adam entered the candlelit kitchen carrying Mallory's rose and Mrs. Trigali's radio that he'd plucked from the foyer table. Mallory, wearing a short pale pink satin robe, stood at the sink, looking out the window.

After setting the flower and radio on the counter, he came up behind her. "What's going on?" he asked, sliding his arms around her waist and nuzzling her neck.

"It's completely dark outside."

"That's called 'night.'"

"No, I mean no lights—no streetlights, no lights on in the neighbors' houses, nothing."

"Oh. That's called a blackout," he murmured, brushing her hair from her nape so he could kiss the vulnerable bit of fragrant skin. And absorb the quiver that ran through her. "You, me, alone in the dark… Talk about the perfect date. If only I'd known, I would have brought over a pair of night-vision goggles."

She turned in his arms and shot him a skeptical look. "Night-vision goggles?"

"The better to see you with, my dear," he said in his best big-bad-wolf impression.

She laughed, then slid from his embrace and reached for the corkscrew on the counter. "While you open the wine, I'll turn on the radio to see if there's any news about the power outage."

He applied himself to the bottle of pinot grigio he'd brought while Mallory fiddled with the dials. Seconds later an announcer's voice filled the kitchen.

"…Technicians are working to restore power, but have not yet announced any estimates as to when the system will go back on line. Police are asking that people avoid driving as traffic signal lights are out, making for hazardous conditions."

"Guess than means I'm going to have to stay for a while," he said, pouring the pale gold wine into the crystal stems she handed him.

"Guess so. Boy, did you luck out, 'cause otherwise I would have pushed you right out the door."

"…We'll continue with updates to keep you apprised of all the latest blackout developments as they become available. We now return to our regular program, *Sensuous Songs and Decadent Dedications*. Give us a call and tell us what song you'd like to hear played for that sensuous, decadent someone. For all you people who are stuck together in the dark, here's a special selection from us to you—'Something to Talk About.' Hey—don't do anything we wouldn't do."

Smiling, he lifted his glass. "Great choice of song. Here's to givin' 'em something to talk about."

She touched the rim of her glass to his. "I think we already have. In fact, I bet Mrs. Trigali and Mr. Finney are talking about us right now."

"No doubt. They're nice people." He sipped his wine, enjoying the smooth slide of subtle flavor down his throat. "I wasn't surprised to discover that you'd have a good relationship with your neighbors. Block captain, are you?" he asked in a teasing voice.

She smiled and nodded. "We all sort of look out for each other." Walking around to the snack bar, she slid onto an oak bar stool and indicated the platter on the counter. "Antipasto. I made it because I figured with having pasta for dinner, the antipasto would cancel out the calories."

He chuckled and it struck him that no other woman had ever made him laugh as she had. Made him feel as relaxed and able to be himself. Of course, that shouldn't surprise him as her sense of humor was one of the many reasons he'd fallen in love with her.

Sliding onto the bar stool next to hers, he said, "Great theory, except now we're not having pasta."

"Still, it never hurts to work up a good sweat…" Her eyes alight with teasing sensual promise, she snagged an olive from the platter and slowly drew it into her mouth.

"I can think of a dozen ways without even trying."

"Then we'd better eat now—to keep up our strength."

She picked up another olive and offered it to him. Lightly grasping her wrist, he drew the olive and her fingers into his mouth. After slowly withdrawing her fingers, he shot her a wink and savored the tart, salty taste on his tongue. "Delicious."

While he chewed, he looked around. The kitchen was cozy, with glossy white cabinets accented with antique brass knobs and a green granite countertop. It led to an eating area with a white tile-topped table and four oak chairs set by a huge picture window looking out into what he guessed would be a small but neat backyard.

"I like your house."

"Thank you. I love this neighborhood. It's a great mix of young families and empty nesters. The homes are small, but that's the only way I could afford to buy—that and the fact that this house was in foreclosure and a real fixer-upper."

"Guess it helps that you're in the business."

"Absolutely. I wouldn't have known about this house otherwise. Even though it needed work, I knew that with the steady increases in the market it was a good investment. With the repairs I've made, its value has already gone up considerably."

"What sort of work did you have done?"

"Mostly plumbing and electrical. Replacing some Sheetrock. Updating the bathrooms and putting in new kitchen cabinets and countertops. Adding this snack bar." She eyed him over the rim of her wineglass. "You know how to do all that sort of stuff don't you?"

"Yes. I like working with my hands." To prove his point, and also because he couldn't seem to keep his hands off her, he reached out and skimmed his fingers up her shapely calf.

"Noted. And very much appreciated. I did all the painting myself."

He glanced at the sunshine-yellow walls and glossy white trim, then nodded. "Nice job."

"Never let it be said that I don't know the business end of a paintbrush."

Drawing lazy circles around her knee with his index finger, he looked around again and realized that this wasn't just a house, it was a home, with little personal touches everywhere, from the leafy plants gracing her windowsill to the pretty patterned curtains, to the grouping of various-size polished oak picture frames filled with family candids hanging on the wall.

"You're happy here," he said. "I'm glad."

"I'm more than happy. I'm…content. Buying this house, settling in one place, has given me the sense of stability I've always wanted. Out of all the places I lived growing up, I loved Long Island the best. It was the place where I lived in a house—even though it was a rented one—for the first time. It was the first place that ever felt like…home." She smiled and popped another olive into her mouth. "And now I finally have the home, the house I've always wanted. No more apartments, no more temporary housing. Heck, I even love mowing my lawn."

His gaze moved to the refrigerator where several drawings, obviously done by a child, decorated the surface.

"Who did the artwork?" he asked, nodding toward the drawings.

She selected a slice of rolled salami and a wedge of cheese. "Emma, the little girl across the street. I watch her occasionally for Bob and Deb—her parents. Emma likes to come here because I always have Rocky Road ice cream in the freezer and Hershey's Kisses in the pantry."

"Good to know." Snagging a bread stick wrapped in Italian ham, he thought about her watching her neighbor's kid, the friendly camaraderie she shared with Mrs. Trigali and Mr. Finney, and an odd yearning filled him. "It's nice that you have such a close relationship with your neighbors. Except to exchange an occasional hello, I barely see any of mine, let alone know them well."

"Maybe that will change now that you're not working such crazy hours."

"Maybe." But he doubted it. There was something about an apartment that just didn't have the same homey quality as a house. Given her upbringing, he could understand why she'd craved owning her own house. Not having that prospect of moving hanging over her head. And it suddenly occurred to him that while his apartment was where he lived, it didn't feel like a *home*. Not like this small, cozy, fixer-upper house of Mallory's.

A frown yanked down his brows. Damn, he was losing his marbles. His apartment was perfect. Sure it was a little sparse as far as decorations went, but it had all the basics a bachelor needed—beer in the fridge, takeout places within walking distance, a comfortable sofa, big-screen TV and a king-size bed. And what difference did it make? He'd be moving in six months when his lease was up.

Deciding to shift the conversation away from domestic stuff, he asked, "What did you say to Mrs. Trigali that had her relocating the meeting?"

"When I told her you and I were getting together for this evening only, she put two and two together and realized four was a crowd."

This evening only...

Those words reverberated through Adam, and in spite of the fact that they were perfectly true, they left behind an unsettling sensation he couldn't name other than to know that he didn't particularly like it. And sizzled impatience through his system to have her again.

Standing, he snagged her hand and gently tugged.

"Where are we going?" she asked, sliding off the stool.

He unknotted the sash of her robe and slipped his hands inside the parted material to run his palms over the enticing curve of her waist.

"Let's take a shower," he said, leaning down to nuzzle her soft, fragrant neck. "I want to make wet, hot love to you in the water. See if it's as good as I remember."

"That sounds lovely. But with the power out, the water might not stay warm for long."

"You have a problem with a wet, hot quickie?"

"Now *that's* a rhetorical question if I've ever heard one."

9

MALLORY STOOD under the warm shower spray, her palms braced against the pale green tiles, her head falling limply between her arms while she luxuriated in the incredible sensations humming through her body courtesy of Adam's soapy hands.

Lifting her head, she peeked at him over her shoulder. "For a guy who claimed he wanted a quickie, you're taking your sweet time." Her muscles turned to warmed wax under his long, slow massage down her back and her neck went limp again.

"I never said I wanted a quickie—this time. Only that I was willing should the water turn cold." His hands came forward to glide over her breasts and tease her nipples. "I'd much rather take my time."

One hand slipped lower and she spread her legs wider for him. "Works for me."

His lips wandered over the back of her neck, along her shoulder, reawakening memories of showering with him. While one hand continued to tease her breasts, the fingers of his other hand eased between her legs to caress her with a lazy, maddening, teasing stroke.

"This beauty mark," he whispered, kissing a spot at the base of her nape. "I remember how I used to love it when you wore your hair up so I could just walk up behind you, like this—" he moved closer and his erection nestled tighter against her buttocks "—and kiss that gorgeous spot."

God, she remembered him doing that. How it thrilled her every time, turning her knees to mush. "I'm surprised you remember," she said, her eyes drifting closed, her senses reeling from the combination of his lips nuzzling her neck and his fingers' slow, relentless arousal of her sex.

"You have another beauty mark—three freckles. Here." His hand brushed under her left breast. "And another one here." His hand curved over her shoulder, then coasted down her back to lightly knead her right buttock.

Flutters ignited in her belly. "You have a good memory."

"It has more to do with you being unforgettable than with me having a good memory."

A small frown pulled at her brows. Unforgettable? Clearly he was only being gallant. If she'd been so unforgettable, why had he wanted them to see other people? True, she'd been on her way to college, he embarking on his Wall Street career, but she hadn't even thought of dating anyone else while they were apart. She'd found everything she wanted—in him. But he'd been adamant. Kind, but adamant. And she hadn't been about to beg. He'd wanted only friendship—fine. She'd buried her hurt and given him what he wanted.

But all thoughts of the past were driven from her mind, along with everything else when his hand curved over her bottom then moved forward over her slick folds. He slipped two fingers into her from behind, while the fingers of his other hand continued their maddening slow circles over her swollen, aroused flesh. Pressing back, she undulated her hips, seeking more, and he obliged her by touching all the right spots in all the right ways.

For several stunning seconds she remained on the precipice, then her orgasm throbbed through her, dragging a long, husky moan from her throat that tapered off along with her spasms into a purr of pleasure.

"Stay right there, just like that," he whispered against her ear, as if she were going anywhere. As if she were capable of doing anything other than fighting to catch her breath. He moved away from her, forcing her to brace her knees so she didn't slither down the drain. A tearing sound roused her enough to glance over her shoulder. Adam, wet and aroused, rivulets of water trailing down his muscular body, was rolling on a condom. He looked up and the scorching fire in his eyes rippled heat down her spine. With his gaze on hers, he clasped her hips and entered her from behind with one long, deep thrust.

For the space of several breathless heartbeats they remained perfectly still and Mallory absorbed the carnal sensations ricocheting through her. Then he rocked against her, touching her deeper. Her eyes drifted closed and she sighed a long *oooohhh* of pleasure. Standing behind her, he stroked her, slowly, surely, withdrawing nearly all the way from her body, only to glide deep again. One hand slid around her, coasting over her abdomen then dipping between her legs, his fingers knowing exactly where and how to touch her throbbing nerve endings.

"Adam…" she gasped, arching her neck, her back, drowning in sensation. Her orgasm inundated her, a convulsive rush of mindless pleasure. He groaned and thrust deeply, and she absorbed his shudders as he took his release.

She'd thought she couldn't move before, but now she realized how foolish she'd been—now that she *really* knew what overcooked spaghetti felt like. Her breathing still ragged, she felt him gently withdraw from her body, heard the shower door slide open then quickly close again as he clearly disposed of the condom. Then felt his hands on her shoulders, gently turning her around until she faced him.

"Don't let go just yet, okay?" she asked, struggling to open eyelids heavy with postcoital languor. "My knees are totally gone, and it's all your fault."

He anchored her against him with one strong arm then lightly brushed his fingertips over her wet lips. "Not letting go," he said softly.

She managed to hike up her eyelids to half-mast. "As I recall you were good in the shower…."

Her words trailed off at his expression. He looked dazed—understandable if his orgasm had hit the same height on the Richter scale as hers—but he also looked…confused? A small frown bunched between his brows, and his gaze roamed over her face, his fingers brushing over her features as if trying to figure out who she was and how she'd ended up naked in the shower with him.

"You okay?" she felt compelled to ask.

His gaze, dark and intense, met hers. Then he blinked and his expression cleared. "About a hundred times better than 'okay.' You?"

She slid her hands up his chest and pulled his head down for a lush, open-mouthed kiss. "Very okay. At least for now. But I've gotta warn you, I'm going to want to do that again."

He ran his tongue over her bottom lip then nibbled on the sensitive skin. "I don't know when I've ever heard better news."

"Doesn't frighten you off?"

"You've got to be kidding."

She leaned back in the circle of his arms and smiled into his beautiful eyes, his dark lashes spiky from the water. "Good. Because the night's still young and it's come to my attention that I have several months of being unfulfilled to make up for."

His eyebrows shot up. "No way."

"'Fraid so." But as gratified as she was by his unmistakable "your boyfriend must have been nuts" expression, she didn't want to think about, let alone talk about Greg. She shot Adam a crooked grin. "Until you arrived this evening, you could sum up my situation in two words—*lonely* and *horny*."

His slow, wicked smile stole her breath. "Lonely and

horny," he repeated, his hands slipping down to caress her bottom. "A very serious condition commonly called *lorny*. Strikes down thousands of unsuspecting people every year. Luckily, I know just the cure."

"How lucky for me."

He gave her butt a playful squeeze. "Me, too. So let's get started."

"Started?"

"Well, hell, you don't think I'm finished, do you?"

"No," she said with a laugh. "But I think we're past the starting point. What's next?"

For an answer, he turned them so that the spray cascaded over their heads and between their bodies. "A quick rinse off."

"Very quick—the water's turning cold."

Amid much laughing and kissing, they quickly soaped each other up then rinsed under the rapidly cooling water. After shutting off the taps, she'd barely squeezed the excess moisture from her hair and wrapped a towel around herself sarong style, when Adam grabbed the flashlight and her hand and led her across the hall into her bedroom.

"Now what?" she asked.

"Now you relax on the bed for a few minutes while I prepare the next step in the 'lorny' cure, which coincidentally, is nearly identical to the 'reassure her she's potently sexy' cure."

"I see. So in other words, you're good for *everything* that's ailing me."

"Yeah. Which makes me one hell of a lucky guy." He brushed his lips over hers then gave her a gentle nudge toward the bed. "Lie down. Relax. I'll be back in five minutes."

Since her knees still felt like mush and lying down sounded really nice, Mallory climbed onto the mattress. Heaving a feminine sigh of pleasure, she watched him leave the room, and decided that no man had ever looked so good wearing nothing except a towel.

Too bad you only have him for tonight, her inner voice whispered.

And in a heartbeat, her sigh of pleasure turned into another sort of sigh altogether.

Yes, too bad she only had him for tonight.

But with him jetting off to parts unknown and the up-in-the-air nature of his future in direct opposition to how she lived her life, tonight was all that the fickle nature of timing allowed them. It was better than nothing. And she had every intention of making the most of their remaining hours. Everything would be fine as long as she didn't forget that she and Adam were, once again, traveling on paths that were heading in opposite directions.

ADAM ENTERED Mallory's kitchen and flicked off the flashlight since the multitude of candles she'd lit provided enough light, as well as scenting the air with the musky, sweet fragrance of vanilla. Then he braced his palms on the cool granite counter, lowered his head and tried to assemble the tornado of emotions swirling through him into some kind of order.

He felt completely...unraveled. Like someone had yanked on a loose string hanging off his shirt and after he'd spun like a top had ended up with no shirt and an untidy mound of thread.

Something was happening here, something between him and Mallory. Something that was a hell of a lot more than just sex. At least it was to him.

He knew all too well what just sex felt like. It was fun, pleasant, lighthearted. Ultimately forgettable. While he supposed *fun* and *pleasant* could be used to describe his evening with Mallory—although both words were a little lukewarm—*lighthearted* and *forgettable* definitely didn't apply.

And that was the problem. This felt…intense. In a way that threw him off balance. In a way he couldn't recall ever experiencing with anyone else.

Except her.

He lifted his head and stared out the window toward the unbroken darkness, seeing nothing save his own dim reflection in the glass. He stared into his own eyes that appeared somewhat dazed. This entire scenario felt so damned familiar. Mallory inundating every corner of his mind. Filling him with laughter and happiness and excitement. And just like before, he found himself feeling too much too soon. And as it had in the past, it scared the hell out of him. He needed to remember this was just for one night. Their only night together. He was Mr. Rebound. A balm for her bruised ego. They each had their own lives that were, once again, veering off in opposite directions. In less than forty-eight hours he'd begin his dream trip. He'd waited a long time for this opportunity—freedom from the pressures and stress of his job, carefree traveling around Europe where he'd enjoy exotic locales, fabulous food, incredible wine, spectacular sights and gorgeous, sexy women.

How was it that a week ago, a day ago, hell—six hours ago, that all had sounded like Utopia and now it sounded like…not Utopia?

Must just be the incredible sex he'd shared with Mallory. Yeah, that's all it was. Apparently she wasn't the only one who'd been "lorny." Not that he'd been lonely. Exactly. Still, all this unexpected and amazing sex had his cylinders out of whack. His hormones out of balance. His red-blood-count levels raised. Once this night was over, once he wasn't being subjected to all this nonstop sexual stimulation, he'd put everything back into perspective.

He was just feeling…nostalgic. Being with Mallory was like being hit with a deluge of memories of the feelings and emotions he'd felt for her years ago. How much he'd enjoyed her company, in and out of bed. Yes, that's all they were—memories.

Whew! See? All he needed was to put some physical space between them for a few minutes to get his head cleared and his thoughts back into alignment. 'Cause damn—how was a guy supposed to think straight when she was kissing him? Touching him? When he was buried deep inside her?

She was on the career track, and he'd just gotten off that treadmill. She needed structure, stability, and his plans for the foreseeable future were anything but. Still, he couldn't shake this feeling that he'd been sucker punched. Right in the heart.

But surely that was just a result of all these memories. Remembering all the things he'd felt when he was with her. The heady excitement. The profound happiness. How much he'd admired and liked her. How deeply he'd loved her. After tonight, they'd go their separate ways, as they'd done in the past. And as it was in the past, it was what was best for both of them.

But before he left, he was going to make damn sure she was plenty reassured and no longer suffering from "lorniness."

He shook his head. How was it that she'd felt unfulfilled for several months? The fact that her ex-boyfriend could manage to keep his hands off her for more than several *minutes*…unbelievable.

But hey, maybe he should send the guy a thank-you note. If not for him being an ass, Adam wouldn't have this night with her. And for this night, she was his.

He spent a few minutes gathering what he wanted, then set up everything on a large acrylic platter with a palm-tree design he found in her cupboard. Just before heading back to the bedroom, he made a quick phone call—remembering to turn off his damn phone when he was finished. Then he picked up the laden platter and walked back to the bedroom.

When he entered, Mallory rolled onto her side and watched with obvious interest while he set the tray on the edge of the bed then removed the thick pillar candles, placing one on the night table and the other on her dresser, casting the room in a pale golden glow.

"What's all this?" she asked, nodding toward the tray.

"Some romantic lighting. The wine. Chocolate candy kisses."

She sat up. "Chocolate kisses? As in Hershey's Chocolate Kisses?"

"Are there any other kind?"

"Not as far as I'm concerned. Raided my pantry, huh?"

"No. I brought them." He held up the large cellophane bag. "Got the extra-large size."

"Fabulous. You can never have too many kisses."

He leaned over and brushed his lips against hers. "My thought exactly. I also brought the music." Straightening, he set the radio on the night table and adjusted the volume.

"…Welcome back to *Sensuous Songs and Decadent Dedications*. Hope everyone is safe during the blackout, and that if you happen to be with someone sensuous and decadent, you're making the most of this opportunity. Give us a call and let us know what song would make your hours in the dark more meaningful. This next song was requested by J.D. in Brooklyn for Kathleen. Hey, Kathleen—your man J.D. says that he hasn't been the same since the minute he laid eyes on you. One look, and his heart was yours. Here's 'Can't Take My Eyes Off of You…'"

With the music playing softly in the background, Adam sat on the bed, close enough so that their knees bumped. He poured two glasses of wine, while Mallory opened the bag of chocolate.

"Wow," she said, unwrapping the silver foil that covered a drop-shaped morsel. "You give orgasms, then provide music, food and drink—and not just any food, but my favorite chocolate? If that's not from some fantasy catalog, I don't know what is. The only thing that could make it better would be if this chocolate was calorie free."

"Glad you're pleased. I've also provided entertainment." He waggled the deck of cards he'd brought.

"You want to play canasta?" She bit her chocolate kiss in half and offered him the other piece. Leaning forward, he clasped her wrist and drew the morsel and her two fingers into his mouth.

After licking the last bit of chocolate from her fingertips, he said, "This is not your standard deck of cards. This is a Truth or Dare deck."

"Uh-oh. I'm not good at that game."

"Why? I never thought you'd have trouble telling the truth."

"Oh, it's not the truth part. It's the dare. I can't do all that 'eat a bug' or 'drink sour milk' stuff."

"Not to worry. This is the Truth or Dare *Lovers' Edition.*"

10

Sunday, 1:00 a.m.

ADAM WATCHED INTEREST kindle in her eyes and he inwardly smiled. When he'd seen the game during his quick shopping trip before driving to her house, he'd figured she would like it. That they *both* would like it.

"Truth or Dare Lovers' Edition," she repeated. "Sounds like fun."

While he shuffled the cards, she fed him another candy kiss then unwrapped one for herself. When he finished mixing the deck, he set it on the bedspread between them. With a grin, he drew the top card. "Ladies first. You want Truth or Dare?"

"Oh, boy. I'll take Truth."

"Chicken," he teased. Holding the card toward the candlelight, he read, "What is the first thing you notice in a member of the opposite sex?"

She pursed her lips and considered. "Depends. If he's smiling, his smile. If he's not, then his eyes."

Some inner devil made Adam say, "Oh, c'mon. You look at his ass first. Admit it."

"Nope. Well, not unless I happen to be behind him,

in which case I guess the ass would come first." She shot a pointed look toward his butt. "Come to think of it, it was the first thing I noticed about you. Your ass looked mighty fine while you were mowing that lawn."

"Thanks. And you noticed my smile next, right?" he teased.

"As a matter of fact, yes. And then, after you took off your sunglasses, your eyes."

"And what did you think?"

Her eyes brimmed with mischief. "You fishing for compliments?"

"No, just the truth." He grinned. "Of course, if the truth happens to be complimentary, I won't complain."

"I liked your smile. It was friendly, yet just a little... naughty. Like you had a good sense of humor and didn't take yourself too seriously. But it was your eyes that really got me."

"Got you how?"

She took a sip of wine, studying him over the rim of her glass while she swallowed. "You really are fishing. I can't be the only woman who's ever told you that your eyes are...lovely."

No, but he couldn't recall the name of even one of those women. He shrugged. "I'm not fishing. I guess I've just never understood what was so great about them. I mean, they do what they're supposed to do and they're blue. Big deal."

"For me, it didn't have so much to do with their color—although I've always liked blue eyes."

"Then what?"

"I don't know exactly how to describe it. I guess it

was a combination of their teasing expression—but teasing in a nice, friendly way—and how they sort of crinkled up at the corners when you smiled. I was the new girl in town and you immediately made me feel at ease. Made me laugh. I suppose the best way to say it is that your eyes were…are…kind."

He sat there, wineglass in hand, without a clue how to respond to her unexpected words. Words that touched him and washed deep pleasure through him.

Before he could think of a reply, she shot him a saucy wink and smiled. "Of course, the fact that they're a bedroomy blue didn't hurt, either." She reached out for a card. "Truth or Dare?"

He took a swallow of wine to wet his dry throat, then said, "Dare."

Her gaze scanned the words and a slow smile curved her lips. "Massage your lover's shoulders for one minute while talking about how much you're enjoying it." Chuckling, she shifted around to present her back to him. "Works out well for me."

"And hardly a hardship for me." Setting his glass aside, he reached out and lightly kneaded her shoulders, smiling when she let out a long sigh of pleasure. In keeping with his dare, he said, "I'm enjoying this because of that sound you make when you like something. That breathy vibration that's sort of a sigh, but deeper. Sexier. Like a growl. And the way your skin feels…so soft. Smooth. Makes me wonder what you put on it to make it feel so good beneath my hands."

He shifted closer and massaged her with a slightly stronger stroke. Her head fell forward and she groaned.

"Now *that's* a sound that could make a man drop everything and devote himself to making you groan like that again. And presenting the back of your neck like this..." He brushed her hair aside and kissed her beauty mark. "Very enjoyable." After dropping another kiss to her fragrant neck he sat back.

"That wasn't a minute already," she protested.

"Actually it was more like two minutes."

"Oh. Darn." With a sigh, she turned around to face him. "You've got great hands."

"You've got great shoulders. Among other things." He smiled and drew a card. "Truth or Dare?"

"Since you called me a chicken last time, I feel the need to recapture my honor. Dare."

Adam scanned the card then shook his head. "Man, you're getting off easy with this one."

"What do I have to do?"

"You're a fashion critic," he read. "Critique your lover's outfit."

She made a great show of slowly looking over the towel wrapped around his hips. Then she cleared her throat. "Dressed in the latest in white terry cloth from Bed, Bath & Beyond, my lover makes those Calvin Klein underwear models look like rank amateurs. The way this particular outfit leaves his chest bare..." Reaching out, she slowly dragged her fingertips over his shoulders then circled them slowly around his nipples. Her fingers continued lower, over his abdomen, to tickle across the skin just above the towel's edge, causing his muscles to spasm involuntarily beneath her feathery caress.

"Very nice," she said in a throaty voice that could only be described as a purr. "As is the way the material hugs his hips and legs." Her hand trailed over the terry cloth, then slipped beneath the material to run up his inner thigh. When she cupped him in her warm hand, he sucked in a sharp breath.

"The easy access to his…attributes is definitely a plus. All in all, a very sexy fashion statement that he wears very, very well."

She slowly withdrew her hand, smiling first at his very obvious erection that tented his towel, then raising her gaze to smile at him.

It took a few seconds to find his voice. "I thought you said you weren't good at this game."

"Maybe I was wrong."

"Sweetheart, there's no maybe about it."

Still smiling, she drew a card. "Truth or Dare?"

"I think I'd better try a Truth this time."

"Finish the poem. 'Roses are red, violets are blue…'"

He didn't even have to think about it. "I want to make love again with you."

She clapped. "Wow, and it rhymed and everything."

"Sure did. Now pay up."

Laughing, she shook her head. "We haven't finished the game."

"Fine. But consider this fair warning—I'm not going to last much longer." He drew a card. "Truth or Dare?"

"Truth."

"Who was the first person to break your heart?"

Her smile faltered, then slowly faded. Her gaze skittered away from his and after what felt like a long and somehow awkward silence but was surely no more than ten seconds, she finally met his gaze and said, "You."

He made no attempt to hide his surprise. *"Me?"*

"You."

"*I* broke your heart."

"Yes. You did."

"When? How?"

"What difference does it make now? I answered the question truthfully, so let's move on."

"It makes a difference because I didn't know. Tell me."

She shrugged. "Let's just say I was pretty crushed when you said you thought we should free each other up to date other people."

A weird hollow feeling invaded his chest. "You were?"

She shrugged again and smiled. "Hey, no girl likes to get dumped."

His eyebrows jerked down in a frown and he stared at her. "I didn't dump you, Mallory."

"No? What else do you call it when your boyfriend says he wants to be *friends?* Wants you both to be free to date other people? It doesn't take a rocket scientist to read between the lines."

"We mutually agreed, given our ages and situations that it would be better to cool things off. Not to tie each other down."

"It was painfully obvious there was more to it than that, Adam. But since that was the only explanation you'd give me, I had to go with it. What you call 'mutually agreed,' I call 'you decided.'"

"But you agreed! Wholeheartedly, as I recall."

"What did you expect me to do? Clearly *you* wanted freedom or you wouldn't have broached the subject. Unless I wanted to come off as desperate and clinging— which I wasn't about to do—I didn't have much choice. I might not have had much pride, but I had a little. I'd already been dumped once that summer by my Chicago boyfriend. Twice was just a bit too much humiliation to take."

"Wait a minute. Your Chicago guy didn't dump you—you broke up with him."

She shook her head. "No. I'd intended to break up with him. Because of my feelings for you. But before I had a chance to tell him, he called me. Told me he'd met someone else. Not that I was heartbroken, or even surprised, but still. But with you...well, I was both."

"Heartbroken? Don't you think that's an exaggeration? I mean, you sure regrouped fast enough."

"Meaning what?"

"Meaning when I called you your second week at school, you were already dating some other guy. You told me how great he was. How much you liked him. What a terrific time you were having together." And even after all these years, he still recalled how deeply her words had hurt.

She nibbled on her bottom lip, then shifted her gaze to look down at her hands. "I might have overstated things a bit."

"What does *that* mean?"

She blew out a long sigh, then raised her head to meet his gaze. "I made him up. I wasn't dating anyone."

He felt as if everything inside him shifted. "You weren't?"

"No. But when you called, the thought of having to listen to the man I loved tell me how many sophisticated women he was meeting at his new high-powered Wall Street job…well, I couldn't stand to hear it. Especially since all I'd done for those two weeks was cry into my pillow. So I beat you to the punch."

He went perfectly still. Had she just said…? "The man you *loved?* You were in love with me?"

She made a self-conscious sound. "I was *crazy* in love with you."

It took him several erratic heartbeats to find his voice. "You never told me that."

"I never said the words. But I tried to show you in every way I could."

He cast his mind back and he realized that she *had* shown him. In dozens of ways. With thoughtful gestures. Home-baked cookies. Handwritten notes. With countless smiles. And with her body…

"Why didn't you just tell me?" he asked, his voice a gruff rasp.

She took several seconds before answering. "I was afraid. Of scaring you off. Of being rejected. Afraid it was too much too soon. Believe me, I was very conscious of our different situations—you'd already graduated college and were starting your career and I'd just graduated from high school. The last thing I wanted was to come off like some lovelorn teenage coed. So I decided I'd just wait for you to tell me first." A ghost of a smile crossed her lips. "Except you never did. Instead

you told me we should be friends and see other people."
She winced. "Ouch."

Before he could say anything, she huffed out a
laugh and shook her head. "I have no idea why I told
you all that. It's not like it matters after all these
years."

"You told me because I asked." But she was right. It
didn't matter after all these years.

Did it?

No, of course not.

Still, he felt like he owed her the same truth she'd
given him. "When I called you at school, Mallory…it
wasn't to tell you how many sophisticated women I
was meeting at my new job."

"Oh? Why had you called?"

"Because I'd realized I'd made a mistake." He raked
his hand through his hair. "That I loved you and was
miserable without you. And that I didn't want to be
with anyone else."

Her eyes widened and even in the dim candlelight he
saw her face pale. "Oh…my. Why didn't you say something when you phoned?"

"What was I supposed to say after you'd waxed po-
etic about your incredible new man?"

She stared at him for several long seconds, looking
stunned and slightly dazed. Then she made a humorless
sound. "Well, I'll be damned."

"Yeah. I'll be damned." His head was spinning, trying to wrap around what she'd told him.

She'd been in love with him. *Crazy* in love with
him. God. He briefly squeezed his eyes shut, experi-

encing a strange sensation that felt like some sort of internal malfunction.

"How long had you been in love with me?" she asked, her voice sounding hoarse.

Since the minute I saw you. Since the first time you smiled at me. From the moment I touched you. "Awhile."

"Why didn't you tell me?"

He shook his head. "Same reason you didn't tell me. What I felt for you, the depth of my feelings, scared the hell out of me."

Reaching out, he took her hands and entwined their fingers. "I'm sorry, Mallory. I didn't realize you cared that much. I should have, but…what can I say? I was an idiot. I thought putting some distance between us would help me get my head back on straight, but all it did was make me was miserable. And then it was too late. I never meant to hurt you."

She swallowed. "Seems like I hurt you, too, and I'm sorry. I swear I didn't claim to have a new guy in order to hurt you. I only did it to protect myself. Because you didn't want me anymore."

Didn't want her anymore. He felt as if he'd been turned inside out. "God. Mallory, nothing could have been further from the truth. The problem was that I wanted you *too* much."

And all he'd accomplished was to break her heart. Hell, it hurt just to think about that. And break his own heart in the process. It hurt to think about that, too. Which was ridiculous. It shouldn't hurt after all these years.

Damn. He wasn't at all sure he was happy to know all this. Especially since the knowledge set up a rapid-fire sequence of questions in his mind, all of which started with the words *what if?*

What if he hadn't suggested they give each other their freedom?

What if she hadn't agreed?

What if he'd told her he was in love with her?

What if—

She lightly squeezed his hands, cutting off his thoughts. Then sliding her fingers from his, she gave a light laugh. "Look at us, so serious and caught up in the past. It all happened so long ago and what's done is done. The good news is that we managed to remain friends. How many former lovers can make that claim?"

He didn't know. He didn't care. All he knew was that he felt...undone. And couldn't shake this profound, disturbing sense that he'd lost something very, very special.

The silence between them was broken by the radio announcer's smooth voice. "Here's the latest blackout update—technicians are working to restore power, but there're still no estimates as to when the system will go back on line. Hopefully you're somewhere you can light a few more candles and make the most of the dark. Give us a call here at *Sensuous Songs and Decadent Dedications* and we'll play something to help you set the mood for seduction. Our next dedication goes out to Mallory from Adam. Mallory, Adam requested this song because it's always reminded him of you." The announcer chuckled softly. "Guess we can all figure out what color eyes Mallory has. Here's Van Morrison's 'Brown Eyed Girl'…"

Mallory stared at the radio and her heart performed a slow somersault. She still hadn't recovered from Adam's mind-boggling confession that he'd been in love with her, had cooled off their relationship not from lack of feeling but out of fear, and now this romantic gesture. She turned toward him and even though she knew he'd requested the song, she asked, "Is this from Adam to Mallory as in from you to me?"

"You know any other Adam and a brown-eyed Mallory?"

"When did you call in?"

"When I went to the kitchen." Without taking his gaze from her, he stood and held out his hand. "Wanna dance? For old times' sake?"

Not entirely trusting her voice, she nodded, then shifted to the edge of the bed and stood. She put her hand in his and he drew her closer, setting their joined hands against his chest and wrapping his free arm around her waist. She skimmed her other hand up and over his shoulder to encircle his neck then closed her eyes and rested her temple against his jaw.

A lump lodged in her throat as she was bombarded with a myriad of memories. Adam holding her just like this, turning his head to brush his lips against her hair. His warm breath brushing past her ear, shooting tingles of pleasure all the way down to her feet. His body touching hers from chest to knee as they slowly swayed to the music.

She leaned back to look at him. His gaze searched hers, intense and filled with those same flickers of confusion she'd seen earlier. And something else she couldn't decipher. Was he experiencing the same unsettling sense of the past as she? Was he asking himself the same "what if" questions that were crazily bouncing around in her mind?

What if instead of agreeing when he'd suggested they give each other their freedom she'd told him she was in love with him?

What if she'd listened to what he'd had to say when he'd called her at college before letting her pride claim she'd started a new relationship?

What if—

"Since the day we met," he said, cutting off her reverie, "I've thought of you every single time I've heard this song."

Swallowing the lump in her throat, she shoved the useless "what if" questions aside. There was no point in dwelling on what-might-have-beens. She forced a smile and what she hoped passed for a lighthearted laugh. "Uh-huh. Me and how many other brown-eyed girls that you've known over the years?"

He didn't smile back. "Just you."

She tried to hold off the thrill that washed through her at his softly spoken admission, but it was like trying to hold back the ocean with a rake.

"Not just because you have brown eyes," he continued, "although that's definitely part of the reason—"

"I kinda figured."

One corner of his mouth quirked up. "But it's also

the words…. They've just always brought such a vivid image of you to mind. Especially the part about making love behind the stadium."

Mallory thought for a second, then shook her head. "We never made love behind the stadium."

"I know. But I always wanted to. One of the many adolescent fantasies you inspired—getting it on with my girl behind the stadium, underneath the bleachers."

"So why didn't you ever bring me there? It's not like the high school was a plane ride away. I would have been happy to indulge you."

"I meant to. But then we…ran out of time."

Ran out of time… The words echoed through Mallory's brain. Yes, they had run out of time back then, just as they would soon run out of time now. This night would end and they'd go their separate ways, a reality she firmly pushed aside. Reality would intrude upon them soon enough. Until then, fantasy was all that mattered. So before they went their separate ways…

A smile curved up her lips. "Let's get dressed."

He gave a short laugh. "*Totally* the opposite of what I was about to say."

She ruffled her fingers through the silky hair at his nape. "If you get dressed, I'll make your fantasy come true."

"If you get naked, my fantasy will come true a lot quicker."

She laughed. "I mean your 'behind the stadium' fantasy. The local high school is only about a quarter mile away." She rubbed her pelvis suggestively against his.

"Let's get dressed, walk over there and take care of this unfulfilled fantasy of yours. What do you say?"

For an answer, he yanked off her towel, then his. "Let's get dressed."

11

Sunday, 2:30 a.m.

WALKING ALONG the dark, quiet street lit by nothing more than the hazy silver glow of moonlight, her fingers lightly entwined with Adam's, Mallory pulled in a deep breath. The air was hot, humid, heavy with moisture, and smelled of cut grass and summer flowers. And the clean, fresh, masculine scent of the freshly showered man walking beside her.

Another wave of memories inundated her, of that magical summer when she'd fallen so deeply in love with him. They'd frequently taken long walks, sometimes in the park, sometimes along the beach. Leisurely strolls, hand in hand, talking about everything and nothing. People they knew. Places they'd been and wanted to visit. Their favorite things and least favorite stuff. Sports. School. Books. Music. Movies. It seemed as if they never ran out of conversation. As far as she was concerned, there hadn't been enough hours in the day to cram in everything there was to say and do.

She'd loved talking to him. Listening to his deep voice. His laugh. His gentle teasing as he tried to convince her that since she was now a New Yorker she needed to switch her baseball allegiance from the Cubs to the Yankees.

Yet she'd also cherished their comfortable silences, the times when they'd just sit, their arms wrapped around each other, and watch the sunset. Or the gulls fight over a morsel left by the day's beachgoers. How she'd close her eyes and lean against him, absorbing the feel of him surrounding her, and think that this was just the beginning of something very, very good.

"Are we almost there?" he asked, yanking her thoughts back to the present.

She inwardly smiled at the hint of impatience in his voice. "Just around this next corner."

"Thank God. Feels like we've been walking for hours."

"It's been about four and a half minutes."

"Well, in my alternate 'dying to get my hands on you' universe, those four and a half minutes feel like an eternity."

There was no denying the delighted shiver of anticipation those "dying to get his hands on her" words rippled through her.

They rounded the corner and the high school came into view, the tall stadium visible behind the building. Adam quickened his step and Mallory practically had to jog to keep up with his long-legged strides.

"Good thing I didn't wear my heels," she said, glancing down at her flip-flops. "What are you, in a rush?"

"A gorgeous, sexy woman who has me so aroused I can barely see straight is going to rock my world as soon as I can get her behind that stadium. Yeah, you might say I'm in a bit of a rush."

When the stadium loomed before them, Adam broke out into a run, tugging her along. Laughing, feeling wilder and freer than she had in a long time, she ran with him across the grass. By the time he pulled her beneath the bleachers, she was gasping for air. Wrapping his arms around her waist, he lifted her up and spun her around until she was dizzy and weak from laughter.

When he stopped, he slowly lowered her, her body dragging along his. Before she could catch her breath, he kissed her. A hot, deep, demanding, impatient kiss that set her on fire until she imagined her every nerve ending glowed. And she realized that *he* was what was making her dizzy. Just as he always had.

Without breaking their frantic kiss, he stepped backward until he bumped into one of the thick cement columns. He immediately turned them, pinning her against the column with his body. And then he simply overwhelmed her, inundating her with a deluge of sensations so rapid she could barely keep up.

His hands were…everywhere. Pushing up her tank top. Cupping her breasts. Teasing her nipples. Skimming over her stomach. Down her legs, then back up, slipping under her skirt.

He broke off their kiss, his breathing a labored growl. "You're not wearing any underwear."

"Is that a complaint?"

"No. God, no." He impatiently yanked down her skirt and she kicked it aside. Gliding his fingers between her thighs, he stroked her with a maddening rhythm that dragged a long moan from her throat—a moan that turned into a gasp of pleasure when he slipped two fingers inside her.

"You feel so good," he said against her lips, his voice a ragged groan. "So wet. So tight. So hot." His mouth blazed a downward trail, kissing, nipping, licking. When his tongue laved her nipple, she arched her back, a plea he instantly answered by drawing the stiffened peak into the heat of his mouth. Each pull of his lips on her breast was matched by a deep stroke of his amazingly talented fingers, the combination of which made her come in a convulsive rush.

Gasping for breath, her shudders had barely subsided when he dropped to his knees before her, spread her thighs wider and ran his tongue along her cleft. Her eyes slid closed as his lips and tongue proved as amazingly talented and relentless as his fingers. With her body still humming with the aftershocks of her last climax, another orgasm rocketed through her, forcing a ragged cry from her throat.

Eyes closed, muscles lax, breathing unsteady, and floating on a hazy cloud of postorgasmic bliss, she was vaguely aware that he stood. Somewhere in the back of her glazed mind she heard the tearing of a wrapper. The hiss of a zipper. Then he lifted her and moved between her thighs.

"Wrap your legs around me," he said, his voice rough with arousal. She clasped her ankles behind him and with a groan he thrust deep. Then slowly withdrew, the erotic pull setting up a deep craving and reawakening nerve endings that only seconds ago she'd thought sated. Another deep thrust, dragging a guttural growl from her to mingle with his, followed by a slow, gliding withdrawal. A thought-destroying rhythm that he repeated. Again. Again. Harder. Faster.

Her hands clutched his shoulders, her thighs tightened around his hips as the tremors started deep in her body, radiating outward in spasms that pulsed hot pleasure through her system. She felt him thrust a final time then bury his face in the space where her neck and shoulder met as his orgasm shuddered through him.

Neither moved for several seconds. His warm breath battered her neck, while she fought to pull air into her lungs, the musky scent of their passion filling her head. She prayed he didn't release her because if he did, she'd just slide to the ground in a steaming lump of melted, quivering female flesh.

After a few more heartbeats, she swallowed twice and managed to find her voice. "Holy cow."

She felt him nod once against her shoulder.

"You know, if you're going to throw me into the deep end, how about tossing out a 'hold your breath' warning?"

He lifted his head and looked at her through glazed eyes. "Couldn't. I got my hands on you and forgot how to speak English."

"Well, that's not good since you're the brains of this outfit now that you've melted mine."

"Great. Maybe now I can beat you at Scrabble."

"Not likely. Which means I'm the brains and you're the brawn."

"No, I'm the brains, you're the beauty. And brains, too."

"Hey, flattery will get you...everywhere."

He leaned forward and lightly kissed her. "Not flattery," he whispered against her lips. "The truth. Beautiful. In every way. Inside and out."

"Well, jeez, if you're going to put it *that* way, my knees aren't going to recover anytime soon."

His arms tightened around her and he rested his forehead against hers. "No problem. I've got you."

Those softly spoken words brushed over her lips and echoed through her mind. *I've got you... I've got you...* And she suddenly realized that she stood in real danger of giving them much more meaning than he'd intended.

He shifted slightly and she unclasped her ankles. Her legs slithered limply down his until her bare feet touched the grass. At some point her flip-flops had fallen off. Probably between climaxes two and three.

"You okay?" he asked.

"What kind of a question is that to ask a woman you just brought to orgasm three times? I'm..." Her voice trailed off as he gently withdrew from her body.

"Beautiful?" he supplied. "Incredible? Sexy as hell?"

"Knee-less is more what I was thinking. Although *incredible* is a pretty apt description."

"Oh, yeah, you're definitely incredible."

"No, I mean I *feel* incredible."

He ran his hands down her body. "Totally agree."

A laugh huffed from between her lips. "No, I mean you made me feel incredible."

He dropped a quick kiss on her lips. "Back at ya, sweetheart. Are your knees okay yet? Can I let go for a minute?"

She wasn't certain, but her pride forced her to say,

"Sure. I'm fine." Then she braced her knees—just in case.

He released her, stepped back, then pulled a tissue from his back pocket. Still feeling as if she were bobbing around in zero gravity, her eyes drifted closed. She heard him step away, presumably to dispose of the condom in the nearby trash can, then the soft glide of his zipper going up. When he didn't return to her after several seconds, she dragged her eyelids open and found him standing about six feet away, his gaze slowly tracking up her body.

When his gaze locked onto hers, the intensity burning in his eyes shot a thrill of feminine power through her. Wearing nothing except her satin tank top, she felt sexy and wanton and deliciously wicked.

Nestling her shoulders more comfortably against the cement pillar, she lifted her arms and slowly sifted her fingers through her hair, watching him through hooded eyes. "So…did I make your fantasy come true?" she asked.

A muscle jerked in his jaw, then he blew out a long, slow breath. Regarding her with a heated look that made her feel as if she stood in a circle of fire, he slowly erased the distance between them until less than a foot remained. Bracing his hands on the pillar, he bracketed her in.

"Make my fantasy come true? Sweetheart, I can't believe you'd even need to ask." A flicker of concern flashed in his eyes. "I didn't hurt you, did I?"

"Sweetheart, I can't believe you'd even need to ask," she said, mimicking his response. Any more than she could believe that arousal was nipping at her again.

"I don't usually…" He shook his head and frowned.

"Don't usually what?"

"Lose control like that."

His admission stilled her. She recalled that he'd often lost control like that with her. With flattering frequency. Just as she had with him. Just as she hadn't in quite the same way with anyone else since.

Walking her fingers up his shirt, she looped her arms around his neck. "I, um, really liked your fantasy."

"That makes two of us. And if you keep looking at me like that, you'll be making my fantasy come true all over again."

She heaved a dramatic sigh. "Yeah, and I'd hate that. Really."

"So now that you know all about my behind-the-stadium fantasy, how about sharing one of yours?"

"Hmm… Mine would involve an unexpected encounter with a well-dressed man. Everything would be very businesslike, but then he'd take off his suit jacket. Unbutton the top button of his shirt and loosen his tie. Roll back his shirtsleeves." She heaved out a sigh. "For reasons I can't explain, that loosened-tie, rolled-up-sleeves look on a man turns my knees to jelly."

"And then what?"

"And then all talk of business would go out the window, I'd bring him back to my place and we'd have a nooner." She grinned. "But your fantasy wasn't too far off from another one of mine."

"Don't tell me—doing it with the captain of the football team?"

"Well, face it. Not too many girls fantasize about doing it with the vice president of the photography club." She bent her knee and rubbed it against his thigh. "Although I'm guessing you easily could have changed that."

"Hey—I didn't need the stadium. I had the darkroom."

"And now you've had the stadium, too."

"I think that makes me all kinds of lucky."

"Funny, I was just thinking it had made *me* all kinds of lucky. Three times."

He waggled his brows. "Wanna go for four?"

"Wow. Forget the amusement park, *this* is the happiest place on earth. Probably wouldn't take much to hit four. I find your presence quite…stimulating. Not to mention I, uh, seem to be without my skirt. Or panties."

"That's a shame. But as I recall, you didn't have any panties to start with."

"Oh. Right. I forgot."

"I don't see how you could forget. I sure as hell never will."

He removed one hand from the column and his fingers slowly traced a line down the center of her torso to tangle in the curls at the apex of her thighs.

Mallory sucked in a quick breath as her libido snapped to instant attention at his gentle, teasing caress over her sex.

He lowered his head and kissed the side of her neck. "You realize I can't keep my hands off you."

"I'm flattered. And…ooooh, yeah, right there… grateful." She slid one hand down his body and rubbed his hard length through his jeans. "I don't suppose you brought *two* condoms?"

"Sure did."

Her soft chuckle turned into a moan as he insinuated his knee between her thighs and spread her legs wider to stroke her with that same relentless perfection that had already sent her over the edge.

She flicked open the button on his jeans and lowered the zipper. "You know we'd be more comfortable in my bed. But I'm thinking we may not get back to the house before dawn."

"I'm thinking maybe you're right. Besides, I'm so unbelievably hard, comfort is kinda secondary at this point."

She slid her hand beneath the waistband of his boxer briefs and wrapped her fingers around him. *Oh, my.* He wasn't kidding about being hard. "Secondary?" she crooned, gently squeezing him. "What's primary?"

"I'm so glad you asked, brown-eyed girl. Because I'd be delighted to show you."

And boy, was she delighted to be shown.

12

Sunday, 4:00 a.m.

SURROUNDED BY DARKNESS, hot, humid air and the music of crickets, they slowly walked, arm in arm, back to the house—after having put the other condom Adam had brought to very good use. They hadn't taken more than a dozen steps before he decided he very much liked the weight of Mallory's head leaning against his shoulder. Liked the way her hip brushed his with their every step. Liked her delicate scent filling his head every time he inhaled. Having only to turn his head to kiss her temple. The soft texture of her hair brushing his chin.

Liked everything about her.

Just like old times.

Being with her felt so damn good. But then, it always had. And not just in a sexual way—although he couldn't name another woman who'd ever aroused him so completely. And so damn fast. Hell, it seemed that all she had to do was look at him and he was hard. And God help him, now whenever he heard "Brown Eyed Girl," he'd have a whole new set of Mallory-induced memories to think about.

But even taking the amazing sex out of the mix, he just liked being with her. He remembered how she'd make him happy just with a smile. Just by standing in the same room with him. She made him laugh, and he enjoyed talking to her. He even enjoyed not talking to her—like now—when they just walked along in silence. An image popped into his mind, of his upcoming European vacation, of the two of them walking like this along the Seine in Paris, or through the cobblestone streets of Rome. Too bad she couldn't come with him—

His footsteps faltered and he sliced that thought right off. What the hell was he thinking? He was only the rebound guy. Besides, talk about a bachelor stylecramper—bringing a woman with him on his vacation.

"Watch your step so you don't fall," she said softly, rematching her steps to his. "The sidewalks aren't always even."

Watch your step so you don't fall. Good advice. Only problem was that he was starting to suspect it was coming a bit too late—and had nothing to do with uneven sidewalks.

Her hip bumped his and she splayed her free hand against his stomach, gently rubbing his abdomen. An oddly contradictory sense of contented peace and undeniable lust coiled through him, and he was inundated with the unsettling notion that maybe his plan to date a string of different women wasn't all it was cracked up to be. That it wouldn't provide him with this same sense of "rightness" being with Mallory gave him. And damn it, try as he might to picture his arm wrapped around another woman, walking with another woman, hell, making love to another woman, all he could see was Mallory. It was as if she were branded on his retinas.

She lifted her head from his shoulder and skimmed her hand over his belly again. "Have you given any thought as to what sort of new career you'd like to try?"

He latched onto the conversational gambit like a lifeline thrown to a drowning man. "Given it a lot of thought, but haven't reached any definite decisions yet. It's come down more to knowing what I *don't* want to do, so I figure I'll get there eventually by process of elimination."

"What are some of the things you don't want to do?"

"Sumo wrestling."

She laughed. "What else?"

"Chef."

"Don't like kitchens?"

"I like them—as long as my being in one doesn't actually involve any cooking."

"You can't cook?"

"I can make coffee. Does that count?"

"What do you eat?"

"I live in Manhattan. No one cooks in Manhattan. Why cook when there're two dozen take-out places within two blocks?"

"So you can't even slap together a peanut-butter-and-jelly sandwich?"

"Well, yeah, I can do that. I can also pour milk on cereal, pop a bagel in the toaster, open a jar of salsa and a bag of chips, and mix a perfect martini."

"And you say you can't cook?" she asked, her voice and expression filled with exaggerated shock. "What other career options have you decided against?"

"Well, I considered being a congressman—but there's all that politics and stuff."

"Hmm. Definitely a drawback. How about a rocket scientist?"

"Nah. All that math and stuff."

"Brain surgeon?"

"All that blood and stuff."

"Farmer?"

"All those cows and stuff."

"I'm beginning to see a pattern here. So opening the tiki bar in Hawaii is really a possibility?"

"Can't say I've ruled it out. The doctor said low stress and it doesn't get more low stress than hanging at the beach, mixing piña coladas. And you can't beat the weather."

"What about photography? You do very well with lingerie-wearing customers."

"I don't think I can top the photos I took of you, so I'm going to rest on my laurels."

"If you get tired of mixing cocktails, what about using your Wall Street experience and being a financial planner?"

"I've thought about it, but after being away from all that for the past few months, I'm just not missing it. I like keeping on top of my own portfolio, but I think I'd rather go for a swim in a completely different type of pool." They turned the corner onto Mallory's quiet street. "Actually, an idea's been tugging at me for the past month or so."

"Besides the Hawaiian tiki bar?"

"Yes. Remember how I told you that I'd finished Nick's basement for him?"

"Yes."

"I really enjoyed doing that, and not just because it was for a friend. It gave me a sense of accomplishment and calm that I hadn't felt in a long time. Sort of got me thinking about starting my own contracting business. Home repairs, adding dormers, finishing basements, updating kitchens and baths—that sort of thing. Not only do I like that type of work, but it's something I could do wherever I decide to live."

She nodded slowly, and he could almost hear the wheels turning in her mind. "I can only speak for here, but with so many older homes on Long Island, there's a great demand for that sort of work. If you decide that's what you want to do in this area, let me know. Buyers and sellers constantly ask me to recommend contractors and I'd be happy to pass your name to them. You wouldn't lack for customers, and word of mouth spreads quickly. I recommended a friend's husband who's a roofer to one person in my mother's neighborhood, and from that job he's gotten half a dozen more."

He looked at her and smiled. "Thanks. I'll keep that in mind."

"You're welcome." She removed her hand from his stomach and he immediately missed the feel of her touching him. The easy intimacy of her caress. Reaching out, he snagged her wrist and set her hand right back where it had been. Ah. Much better.

Her expression turned serious, and she said, "I just thought of something else you might want to consider."

"Like speeding up this walk so I can get you naked again?"

She laughed. "I think if I looked up *insatiable* in the dictionary I'd see your smiling face. What the heck kind of vitamins do you take?"

"It has nothing to do with vitamins and everything to do with you." He pulled her to a stop and kissed her. He'd meant it to be a quick, playful kiss, but it instantly turned into a deep, lush, tongue-mating exchange that made even his lungs feels hot—like he was breathing in steam.

When he lifted his head, he looked into her eyes that resembled glazed chocolate and for the second time in minutes felt like a drowning man.

"Whew," she said, resting her forehead against his chin. "If I'd had any idea stockbrokers could kiss like that, I definitely would have considered investing in the market. And I sure as heck wouldn't have been wasting my time with lawyers."

He knew she was kidding, but the thought of her kissing some other stockbroker cramped his insides with an unpleasant sensation he recognized all too well as jealousy. And as for her dirtbag lawyer ex, the thought of that cheating creep so much as touching her made him want to break something—like the cheating creep's face. Damn, if someone like Mallory was his, he'd never touch another woman—

He squeezed his eyes shut to sever the thought.

Oh, boy.

Let's be totally honest here, dude, his inner voice piped up. *This isn't about not touching another woman if "someone like Mallory" was yours.* And he couldn't deny it. No, the unvarnished truth was that if *Mallory* was his, he'd never touch another woman. He'd never want to.

Yet the confusing thing was that the thought of Mallory being his didn't even remotely fill him with the sort of this-could-royally-screw-up-my-plans panic it should. No, instead it suffused him with a sort of warm, tingly glow. A deep yearning unlike anything he could ever recall feeling before. And the fact that that warm, tingly, glowy yearning didn't fill him with panic…

A low groan escaped him.

"You okay?" she asked, and he felt her lean back.

He opened his eyes. One look at her irrevocably confirmed that he had one foot dangling over the edge and the other precariously balanced on a banana peel. Now he just needed to decide what the hell he planned to do about that.

"I'm great," he said. He dropped a quick kiss on her nose, then started walking again, keeping his arm around her. "But I'll be better once I have you naked again." Oh, yeah, good plan. 'Cause having her naked really helped his decision-making processes.

"You know, before you whiplashed my brain cells into next week with that kiss," she said, "I'd mentioned that I'd thought of another career option you might want to consider."

"What's that?"

"Buying and reselling fixer-uppers. Houses that need substantial repairs, not just new carpeting and a coat of paint. Or in some cases, houses whose interiors—mostly the kitchens and bathrooms—are just way outdated. I've sold many a house that would have gone for tens of thousands of dollars more if they'd been in good condition or updated. Someone who could do those sorts of repairs could buy the house, fix it up for a fraction of the cost of hiring contractors, then resell it at a profit."

He mulled over the idea as they walked along. "Interesting. What sort of profit margin are you talking about?"

"On Long Island—just off the top of my head, I'd say that a twenty- to twenty-five-thousand-dollar investment in a new kitchen and bathrooms would translate into a minimum forty-thousand-dollar increase in the resale value of the home."

His brows raised. "Not a bad return. Have you ever considered buying one of these properties yourself and reselling it?"

"I'd love to, but at this point, it's just not feasible. For one thing, the profit margin would be less for me because I'd have to hire out the work, although it would still be attractive enough to make me consider it. But the big stumbling block is that I don't have the capital. A few years down the road, once I've built up more equity in my house that I can borrow against, I'll reassess the situation. But since you have the three necessary ingredients, you might want to think about it."

"Three necessary ingredients?"

"Yes. You have the time, the talent, and although it might be presumptuous of me, I'm guessing the money."

"How do you know I'm not bankrupt?"

Her shoulders raised in a shrug. "Because I've never

known you to be irresponsible. I can't imagine you leaving your job, taking extended trips abroad, unless you'd carefully planned your finances to afford doing so."

He hugged her closer, his hand grazing the soft outer curve of her breast. "Now that's what I like about you—your brain."

"Uh-huh. Are you aware that *brain* is not a secret code word for *breasts?*"

He laughed and brushed his hand over her breast again, deliberately this time. "I guess I know now."

A grin curved her lips. "Besides, I read the business section of the newspaper. I have a clue as to how much a seat on the stock exchange sells for."

He grinned back. "Maybe I owe all that money to my bookie."

"Maybe." Mischief danced in her eyes. "Have you thought about maybe being a bookie?"

"Nah. All those odds and stuff."

"Ah. Well, think about what I said. Let me know if you're interested."

"Okay." He would. But right now, what he was interested in was getting her back to her house. And getting her naked. Thankfully her house was just ahead.

After closing and locking the front door behind them, Adam led her directly into the bathroom where he turned on the shower.

"I think I have grass stains on my ass," he said, pulling his shirt over his head.

She grinned and stripped off her wrinkled top. "I did offer to be on the bottom, you know."

His avid gaze traveled over her full breasts, and he couldn't stop himself from leaning down to playfully swipe his tongue over one velvety nipple. When he straightened, he started on his jeans and said, "A gentleman always allows the lady to be on top when either grass or sand are involved."

"Ah. Good to know." She kicked off her flip-flops then slipped off her skirt. "If it makes you feel any better, I have grass stains on my knees."

"I can't say it makes me feel any better *now,* but it sure as hell did at the time." He held up his discarded jeans and pointed. "You'll note I have grass stains on my knees, too."

She shot him a wicked grin over her bare shoulder as she stepped into the shower. "And I thank you from the bottom of my heart." Her words were followed by a sharp intake of breath and a yelp. "Yikes! This water is *cold.*"

He stepped in behind her and sucked in a hissing breath as the chilly spray hit him in the chest.

"I vote we make this quick," she said slapping a bar of soap against his stomach and reaching for the shampoo.

"Then get something to eat," he added. "I'm starving."

Much as he loved being wet with her, he had to agree. Ten minutes later they headed toward the kitchen, Mallory dressed in a pink tank top and white shorts, while Adam wore his boxer briefs. She held the radio, which she set on the counter. She turned the knob and music drifted from the speaker, the song advising listeners to "Love the One You're With."

"Whew, it's hot in here," she said, waving her hand in front of her face. "The AC's loooong gone."

"First the water's cold, now the house is hot," he teased. "I think I sense a bit of the complainer in you."

She turned toward him and gave him an exaggerated ogle that stirred up considerable interest in his underwear. "My complaint with the cold water was that it cut our shower shorter than I'd have liked. My complaint with the house being hot is...well, I guess that's just a complaint. Help me open some windows?"

"Sure. Not that there's any cool air outside, but if a breeze happens by, maybe we'll catch it."

After they'd opened the windows, she snagged two bottles of water from the dark fridge and tossed him one. After taking a long, cool drink, he sat on one of the oak chairs at the kitchen table and tugged her onto his lap.

"I thought you were hungry," she said.

He nuzzled her fragrant neck. "I am."

"I have something that will cool you off." She ruffled her fingers through his hair and shifted her bottom.

"That's not going to cool me off, sweetheart."

With a laugh she rose and walked into the kitchen. When she returned she handed him a spoon and set a carton on the table.

"Ice cream," she said, pulling up a chair next to him.

He looked at the label. "Rocky Road. One of my favorites."

"Figured we should eat it. Not only is it cold, but it'd be a shame to let it melt if the power stays out a long time."

"Absolutely. Glad you thought of it. Besides, I suspect we could use the calcium boost." He smiled and grabbed her hand before she could sit on the other chair and tugged her toward him. "Did you know ice cream tastes better when eaten while sitting on someone's lap?" He waggled his brows. "C'mere, cutie, and bring your spoon."

With a devilish sparkle in her eyes, she faced him then straddled his legs, settling herself on his thighs. He clasped her hips and shifted her closer, so that his erection nestled right where she'd feel it best.

He ran his hands in slow circles around her buttocks and smiled. "Care to feed me a spoonful? My hands are busy."

Holding the carton between them, she scooped out a generous spoonful. But instead of offering him the morsel, she slowly drew the spoon into, then out of, her mouth. He felt his eyes glaze over.

"Delicious," she said.

"Do that again."

"Don't you want some?"

"Are we still talking about ice cream?"

"We are," she said in a prim voice that in no way matched the seductive curve of her lips.

"Later. Right now I'm much more interested in watching you."

She scooped up a bit more and obliged him. The sight of her lips wrapped around that spoon pulsed heat straight to his groin.

"That look you're giving me is melting my ice cream," she said.

"Your fault. You're making me hotter than hell."

"Then let me cool you off." She ate another spoonful of ice cream, then leaned forward and brushed her chilled tongue over his lips. "Cooler?" she whispered.

"Not exactly." He licked his lips. "But you taste delicious."

Without a word, she took another mouthful of ice cream. This time when she leaned forward, he cupped the back of her head and brought her closer, kissing her deeply. The cold, sweet, chocolaty silk of her mouth was a stunning contrast to the inferno raging through him.

Damn, how many more jolts could his system take? This woman could arouse him with nothing more than a look. The slightest touch. He sure as hell didn't stand much of a chance against a hot ice-cream kiss.

Breaking off their kiss, he took the carton and spoon from her. "My turn," he said. His gaze wandered down to her chest and he pointed to her tank top with the spoon. "Pretty as it is, that's got to go."

"Oh? And what would my cooperation be worth to you?"

"Take off your top and I'll show you."

Crossing her arms, she grabbed the ends of her shirt and slowly lifted the stretchy material over her head, sinuously moving her body as if performing a striptease. After dropping the top to the floor, her eyes gleamed with sensual challenge. "So show me."

Adam reached out and slowly traced the convex curve of the spoon around her breasts. Her nipples tightened, beckoning him, and she shifted restlessly against his erection.

"You're staring," she said, sounding a bit breathless.

He raised his gaze to hers. "The view is spectacular."

Scooping up a generous spoonful of Rocky Road, he let the ice cream slowly melt in his mouth. Then he leaned forward and drew her nipple into the chill.

Mallory gasped, a shiver of pleasure racing down her spine as Adam swirled his cold tongue around her sensitive peak. Combing her fingers through his thick hair, she arched her back, wanting more. He obliged her, then after eating another spoonful of ice cream, he lavished the same incredible sensations on her other breast. Each icy pull of his lips, each chilled swipe of his tongue, shot a stunning contrast of heat to her core.

Unable to remain still, her hands coasted over his bare shoulders, down his back, his arms, his chest, while she moved her hips, rocking her aching feminine flesh against the hard length of his erection.

"Hold on to me," he said, his voice a husky rasp. She immediately grasped his shoulders and hooked her ankles behind him while he set the container on the table. In one smooth, strong move he rose, and a tingle of anticipation ran through her at the prospect of heading toward the bedroom. But instead of heading down the hallway, he sat her on the table.

"Lay back," he said in that same husky rasp. With her gaze locked on his, her heart pounding at the intensity and arousal glittering in his eyes, she leaned back, bracing her forearms on the oak table.

Without a wasted motion, he stripped off her shorts and panties. Then he hooked her bent knees over his shoulders and slowly, deliberately reached for the ice cream. She watched him take a healthy spoonful into his mouth, then lower himself to his knees.

The sight of her splayed legs draped over Adam's broad shoulders, his dark head between her thighs, speared desire through her. His cold mouth settled on her hot flesh then his chilled tongue thrust into her heated core. Her gasp of pleasure at the shocking contrast melted into a long moan of purring delight.

His tongue and lips stroked and teased until her orgasm was rapidly approaching, but then he leaned back. "Not yet," he said, shaking his head and reaching for the container.

Easy for him to say. But seconds later, he started the magic all over again, his cold mouth and tongue pulsating the most exquisite sensations through her. This time when he brought her to the edge, he didn't stop, and her climax swamped her.

She collapsed onto her back, gasping for breath while delightful aftershocks trembled through her. When she opened her eyes, Adam's face loomed before her. Without a word—because who could talk yet?— she took his face between her hands and kissed him. A long, slow, luxuriously deep kiss that tasted like him and her and chocolate.

When she ended the kiss, she touched her forehead to his. "Guess what I'm going to think about every time I eat ice cream from now on?"

His warm huff of laughter feathered across her lips. "Probably the same thing I'm going to think about."

"Is there any ice cream left?"

"Yeah. Why? You want some more?"

"Oh, yeah." She ran her hand down his chest then trailed a single fingertip down the length of his erection. "Only this time, it's my turn to have dessert. Let's see how you like it."

"Sweetheart, I can't wait to find out."

13

Sunday, 9:00 a.m.

LYING ON HER SIDE, Mallory came awake slowly, each of her senses stirring to life to discover something lovely. And realized that Adam was the cause.

His body spooned snugly behind hers, surrounding her, his skin touching her from her shoulders to her feet, his strong arm wrapped around her waist. His large hand curved over her breast. His deep, even breaths warming the back of her neck.

She blinked her eyes open. Ribbons of sunshine filtered through her sheer cream curtains, which ruffled with a slight breeze. Birds chirped and the crescendo rattle of cicadas floated in the air. She inhaled and smelled a hint of bacon. Which meant that Mr. Finney had fired up his cast-iron grill for his usual Sunday breakfast.

Her gaze tracked around the room, noting her unlit digital alarm clock, indicating the power was still out. Her gaze continued, passing over the candles they'd blown out, then resting on the empty ice-cream container. A flood of sensual memories washed over her and her lips curved upward.

Last night had been...incredible. She'd wanted Adam to reassure her, to help her get her groove back, and he'd succeeded on every level, and then some. Not only had he given her almost more pleasure than she could stand, but his undeniable reaction to her had filled her with a sense of empowerment she'd only ever experienced once before—and that was with him. The fact that their lovemaking was as explosive now as in the past, that she still turned him on as much as he did her amazed and delighted her. That she could make him lose control, could excite and arouse him to that degree...well, she'd certainly never had that effect on Greg.

Her gaze fell on Adam's jeans and shirt haphazardly draped over the chair in the corner, and it hit her that she liked the way they looked there. Liked the feel of waking up with him. Just as she'd liked the feel of falling asleep in his arms. Very much. Too much.

Don't get used to it, her inner voice warned.

Right. Because he was leaving tomorrow. Would be gone for three months on his sojourn across Europe where he'd meet dozens of interesting, sophisticated, gorgeous, exciting women who would no doubt be delighted to show him the sights—and anything else he'd care to see. Maybe he'd love it so much, he'd just stay over there. It wasn't as if he had a house or job here to tie him down. Maybe he'd open his tiki bar on the French Riviera instead of Hawaii. Maybe he'd find the woman of his dreams in Europe.

Her heart stuttered at that thought and she fought to beat back the wave of jealousy that threatened to drown her. When she'd buried the emotion, it was immediately replaced by a dose of self-directed annoyance.

What on earth was wrong with her? This interlude with Adam was a one-nighter. Nothing more. Good grief, she was probably the one hundredth woman who'd wanted to sleep with him—this week alone. The same timing problem that had plagued them in the past still applied—they were heading in opposite directions, both personally and professionally.

Still, she couldn't deny the extraordinary way he'd made her feel. And not only with his lovemaking, although on a scale of one to ten, he'd rated a 5,867. She'd enjoyed talking with him. Walking beside him. Laughing with him. Just as she always had. Being with him had filled her with the same heady, breathtaking, intoxicating excitement she'd experienced during their previous affair.

Yet surely all these warm, fuzzy feelings were simply the result of great sex. Nostalgia. Reboundits. What woman who'd just discovered her boyfriend cheating on her wouldn't dream of having a sexy guy like Adam swoop in to bandage her wounded pride with a night of unbridled sex?

But had he swooped in? Actually, no. *She'd* approached *him*. Not that he'd been at all unwilling, but still, last night had occurred at her initiative. Which made her question her motives. *Why* had she approached him? Was it only to assuage her battered pride? Or was it to exact some sort of revenge on Greg? Or to act on every woman's fantasy that when she gets cheated on she can have a man at her calling? Or had it just been an impulse?

What difference did it make? He was leaving tomorrow and would no doubt promptly forget all about her and their night together as soon as he boarded the plane. His unsettled future plans were just the sort that made her queasy. Her life and career were right where she wanted them.

He may be leaving, but he'll be back, her inner voice slyly reminded her.

Yeah, probably with some exotic supermodel glued to his side. And then he'd be jetting off to some other far-off locale, planning to relocate to God knows where. She wasn't about to put her life on hold even if he asked her to—which he hadn't.

No, she and Adam were like two trains traveling in opposite directions who'd just happened to stop briefly at the same station before continuing on their separate journeys.

He stirred behind her, and his arm tightened around her waist, his fingers flexing on her breast. She heard him inhale then he nuzzled the back of her neck with his warm lips, while his morning erection nestled more firmly against her bare buttocks. With a smile, she reached back and ruffled his hair.

"Good morning," she whispered. "Or is it good afternoon?"

"Uh-oh," he said in a sleep-husky voice. "A pop quiz. And I didn't study." With a smooth motion, he rolled her onto her back, then settled himself on top of her, bracing his upper body on his forearms.

She looked up at him, his blue eyes still hazy with sleep, his dark hair mussed and spilling onto his forehead, whiskers darkening his jaw. He looked decadent and delicious, like a man who'd spent the night making love then falling into exhausted slumber after the last orgasm was fired.

Brushing back his hair, she huffed out a short laugh. "How is it that a man wakes up as good-looking as when he went to bed, but a woman somehow deteriorates during the night?"

His gaze roamed over her and he shook his head. "No deterioration on you, sweetheart. In fact, you're even more gorgeous." He lifted his head and sniffed the air. "And you smell like bacon. God, I've died and gone to heaven."

"That's not me. It's Mr. Finney. He cooks up a full breakfast on his grill every Sunday morning. Bacon, eggs, pancakes. I have a standing invitation, one which includes bringing a guest."

"Tempting. But the bacon's not ready yet, and, um, I am." He gave her an exaggerated leer and a suggestive nudge with his hip.

She bit the inside of her cheeks to keep from laughing. "Don't tell me you're all ready already."

"Okay." He rocked against her again, shooting sparks of pleasure through her. "But something tells me you're going to come to that conclusion all on your own." He bent his head and slowly drew her nipple into his mouth.

"Hmm. How do you know the bacon isn't ready yet?"

"My keen sense of man-smell," he said, his voice vibrating against her breast. "I know fully cooked bacon when I smell it, and that bacon has another…" he lifted his head and sniffed "...at least another four minutes to go."

"Oh, good," she said, reaching for a condom. "And here I thought we'd be rushed."

TWENTY MINUTES LATER, fresh from a very delicious orgasm and a very fast, very cold shower, Mallory and Adam walked up Mr. Finney's driveway.

"Let's not stay too long," Adam said in a low voice. "I feel my second wind coming on."

"Second?" Mallory asked, trying not to laugh. "I think you're on at least your fourth or fifth wind. We can't just eat and run."

"I really think we'll have to. I'm discovering that when it comes to you, I'm sharing impaired."

Before Mallory could think up a reply to that startling statement, they'd arrived at the cedar gate leading to the backyard. Mr. Finney, busy at the grill and wearing a festive red apron emblazoned with the slogan Kiss the Cook over his tropical-print shirt, caught sight of them and motioned them in with a pair of tongs.

"Good morning," he said, his face lighting up with a smile. "You're just in time for breakfast."

Surrounded by air redolent with the smoky flavor of bacon, they walked across the deck to the grill. After exchanging greetings, Mallory held up the bag she carried. "We brought eggs, sausages and bagels."

"Great. I'll put them on the grill. Make yourselves at home. We're having mimosas."

"We?" Mallory asked, setting down the bag near Mr. Finney.

"Sophia and I."

Mallory peeked at Adam over her shoulder, raised her eyebrows and silently mouthed *Oooooh...Sophia?*

At that moment, the back screen door opened and Mrs. Trigali stepped from the house onto the deck.

"Good morning, Mallory, Adam," she said, her face wreathed in smiles. "I see you survived the blackout. Would you like a mimosa?"

"That sounds lovely," Mallory said, smiling in return. "I'll help you." She looked at Adam then pointed to the bag of eggs, sausages and bagels. "Men cook with fire on grill while women prepare festive drinks."

"Okay, but I did warn you that I don't know how to cook."

"Oh, Ray will show you," Mrs. Trigali said, nodding toward Mr. Finney, who was turning slices of bacon. "The man's done nothing but brag about that grill all morning. 'This baby can do anything,' he says. Ha! I say. If it could vacuum and do dishes, then I'd be impressed."

"I'll check it out," Adam said, shooting them a thumbs-up.

Mrs. Trigali took Mallory's arm and led her to the patio table in the far corner where a carafe of orange juice and an open bottle of champagne stood.

After taking two plastic cups from the supply on the table, she looked at Mallory over the edge of her bifocals. Then she smiled and said in an undertone, "No need to ask how your evening with Adam went, my dear. You're practically *glowing*."

"We had a nice time," Mallory managed to say with

a straight face, although obviously the heat scorching her cheeks gave her away. Sitting in one of the patio chairs under the large umbrella, she handed Mrs. Trigali the carafe of orange juice. "How did the block captains' meeting go?"

To Mallory's surprise, Mrs. Trigali's face turned bright red. "It was…fine."

"Oh, boy. Did you and Mr. Finney argue?"

"Not…exactly." She turned toward Mallory and bit her lip. Then she said in a rush, "As a matter of fact, we got on rather well together."

"You did? Well, that's great."

"I taught him how to play canasta. He's really awful, but since I like to win, that worked out fine. Then he taught me how to play poker. I won at that, too, but he claimed it was only beginner's luck and he'd win next time."

"Next time? That sounds promising. I must admit I was surprised to see you here for breakfast."

Mrs. Trigali lifted her chin. "A woman's gotta eat."

Mallory laughed, but her amusement faded as her gaze riveted on Mrs. Trigali's neck. She cocked her head to get a better view, then her eyebrows shot up. "Why, Mrs. Trigali," she whispered, "is that a…*hickey?*"

Mrs. Trigali's hand immediately fluttered to her neck and her blush deepened. "Oh, dear. I *told* him to have a care, but heavens, who'd have thought that a man who was such a pest could kiss so well?" She leaned toward Mallory and confided, "I've decided that I misjudged him. He's not such a pest after all. And he's *very* fond of my cherry lip gloss."

At that moment Mr. Finney looked toward them from the other side of the deck where he stood in front of the grill with Adam. He sent Mrs. Trigali a broad wink and she fluttered her fingers at him in return.

Mallory smothered a laugh. "I'm glad you two have become, um, better friends."

"Well, it's all the fault of the blackout, my dear. Being alone with someone in the dark can put things in an entirely different light—so to speak." She handed Mallory her mimosa then sat down across from her. "Did a night alone in the dark with Adam change your mind about not seeing him again?"

No, her better judgment shouted. *Yes,* her heart hollered. She sipped her drink, then shook her head. "We had a great time, but nothing's changed."

Mrs. Trigali reached out and patted her hand. "I'm sorry, dear. You two seem so well suited. Life's a dance—you should find a partner."

"True. But I need to choose a partner who enjoys the same type of music I do."

"I suppose. But half the fun is learning new dance steps. I sense some fireworks between you and your Adam."

Your Adam. How was it that two simple words could make her feel so unsettled? "So do I. And I don't like it."

"Why not?"

She heaved a sigh. "Because I don't want to get burned."

Mrs. Trigali nodded slowly. "I understand. When I first met my Lou, he made my heart beat fast and my knees feel like overcooked pasta. It was thrilling, yet almost frightening. Luckily I don't scare easily, and for forty years that man weakened my knees. Never forget, my dear, that life isn't measured by the number of breaths we take, but by the moments that take our breath away. If this young man takes your breath away, think twice before you let him get away."

A lump formed in Mallory's throat and she sipped on her drink to dispel it. "Adam's made a number of plans for his immediate future that make it impossible for us to get together anytime soon, if ever."

Mrs. Trigali waved her hand. "You can't expect that it would easy, Mallory. Remember a woman's rule of thumb—if it has tires or testicles, you're going to have trouble with it. No man is easy. It's just that some are worth the effort."

Tires or testicles? Mallory choked back a laugh and nodded. "I'll keep that in mind."

She was saved from further comment when Adam and Mr. Finney approached the table bearing two heaping platters of food.

"That grill is incredible," Adam said, sitting down next to Mallory. "Like something out of a restaurant. With that large, flat cast-iron cooking surface, I've never seen anything like it. I made the scrambled eggs," he said, sounding extremely proud.

"Those crispy black ones?" Mallory teased.

"Ha. Taste this." He held a forkful of fluffy yellow eggs to her lips.

"Delicious," she said after she swallowed the sample. "You're a regular Emeril."

"Who?"

Everyone laughed, then filled their plates. Talk turned to the blackout and speculation as to when the power might come back on.

"Last I heard on the radio was they were hoping everything would be back to normal by this afternoon," Mr. Finney said.

The back gate opened and several more neighbors arrived bearing food. "Hey, Ray," said Bill Porter who lived across the street, "got room for a few more? We come bearing Danish and doughnuts."

"The more the merrier," Mr. Finney said, waving them in.

After performing quick introductions to Adam, Mallory rose and said, "You can take our seats. Adam and I need to get going."

"So soon?" Mr. Finney said.

"I'm afraid so," Mallory said. "I have to call the clients I was supposed to meet today and figure out what we're going to do. Thank you for breakfast. It was delicious."

"Same time, next Sunday," Mr. Finney said, saluting them with his grill tongs. "I'll give you another lesson, Adam."

An odd look passed over Adam's features, but was gone so quickly Mallory wondered if she'd imagined it. "Thanks, but I'll be away."

"Oh, right," Mr. Finney said. "The trip you mentioned. Well, maybe when you get back. The invitation is open."

"Thank you."

They said their goodbyes, then departed through the gate leading toward the driveway. After closing the gate behind them, Adam clasped her hand, entwining their fingers.

"Good breakfast," he said, patting his stomach with his free hand.

"Very good."

"And enjoyable company, although your exit strategy came at the perfect time."

"Actually it wasn't a strategy. I really do need to call the clients I have appointments with this afternoon and check in at my office. Realtors don't get Sundays off."

Adam didn't need a magnifying glass to read the fine print beneath her words, and disappointment rushed through him. Keeping his voice perfectly neutral, he said, "So I guess that means you'll want me to get going."

"I'm afraid so. But you know what they say about all good things."

Yeah. They came to an end. Who the hell had made up *that* crappy rule?

"Besides," she continued, "I'm sure you have a lot to do before leaving on your trip tomorrow."

He did. Laundry. Packing. Putting stops on his mail and newspapers. Dropping by Nick's place to give him spare keys to his apartment and car. Lots of little details. All of which he'd been looking forward to in anticipation of his trip. None of which he now had any desire to do.

That's because you're not currently thinking with your big *brain, man,* his inner voice said with a smirk.

Very true, that.

But surely as soon as he got away from this woman he'd feel differently and his enthusiasm for his trip would return. It was just the sex that was messing with his mind. And making him reluctant to get away from her.

"Did you pick up on the vibe between Mrs. Trigali and Mr. Finney?" she asked, pulling him from his thoughts.

"Oh, yeah. Hey, you don't think we were only talking about bacon and eggs over at the grill, do you?"

She turned her head to look at him and raised her brows. "Actually, yes, that's what I thought. What else did you talk about?"

He shook his head, giving her his best regretful look. "Sorry, babe. Male confidences exchanged over grilling meats are sacred."

"You're joking."

"I'm not."

"How would you know this? By your own admission, you don't know the first thing about grilling meats."

"It's instinctual to the male of the species. Laws of nature, laws of the jungle and all that."

"Uh-huh." They arrived at her house and after closing the door behind them, she leaned against the oak panel and kicked off her flip-flops. "I have ways of making you talk."

Cocking an eyebrow at her discarded footwear, he asked, "You planning to smack me with a flip-flop?"

"Oh, no." She shot him a blatantly suggestive look

that traveled upward from his feet, lingering on his crotch, before finally meeting his gaze.

He crossed his arms over his chest in an effort to look fierce but was really to keep him from grabbing her, and narrowed his eyes. "Are you suggesting that you think you can simply exert your feminine wiles upon me and I'll spill my secrets?"

"I'm not suggesting it—I'm flat-out saying it."

"Ha. I'd like to see you try."

"If I *did* try, you'd fold like a house of cards."

In a heartbeat. "No way."

"You're really tempting me to prove you wrong."

He slanted a crooked grin at her. "I'm trying my best."

"In that case, I'd hate to disappoint you…" With her gaze steady on his, she slowly unbuttoned her sleeveless top, then let the garment slide off her arms and fall to the floor.

Forcing himself to remain still and not erase the arm's length distance between them, he watched as she reached behind her and unhooked her lacy pale blue bra. His gaze tracked the path of the thin straps sliding down her arms and the bra falling to the floor to land on top of her shirt. She then settled her shoulders against the door and skimmed her hands slowly down her body.

He felt his vision blur. A muscle ticked in his jaw as he watched her cup her breasts, teasing her nipples into hardened peaks.

Her gaze dropped to the very obvious bulge behind the zipper in his jeans, a look that felt like a caress, and affected him as surely as if she'd touched him.

Then he damn near forgot how to breathe when she glided her hands down her torso and slowly shimmied her shorts and panties down her legs. After flicking the clothes aside with her foot, she leisurely straightened, tracing her splayed fingers back up the length of her body.

"Are you ready to give up your secrets?" she asked, dragging a fingertip over her nipple.

"Sure. As soon as I can think straight again."

Reaching out, she hooked her index finger into the waistband of his jeans and pulled him closer, until his pelvis bumped hers.

"That's not going to help me think straight, sweetheart."

Tunneling her hands into his hair, she slid her leg up his and hooked her thigh over his hip, then dragged his head down for a lush, intimate kiss.

Damn, neither was that.

With a deep groan, his arms went around her, crushing her to him, his tongue deeply exploring her luscious mouth while his hands explored her soft, fragrant skin. Somewhere in what small portion of his brain she hadn't liquefied, it occurred to him that after they made love it would be time for him to leave. Which meant that this was the last time. *The last time.*

Need clawed at him, his body screaming as if he hadn't touched her in months, and he ached to simply yank open his jeans and bury himself in her wet heat. But they needed a condom, and damn it, they were in the bedroom. Bending his knees, he scooped her up and headed swiftly toward the hallway, making a mental vow never to approach her again unless he had a condom within reach. Better make that two. Okay, three.

Two or three isn't necessary, his inner voice whispered, *since this is the last time.*

That reminder brought on an ache of an entirely different sort, one he could neither name nor wished to examine right now.

"Your conversation at the grill?" she prompted, brushing her lips against his neck.

"You're expecting a lot from a guy who can barely form a coherent thought—your fault by the way."

"Just give me the condensed version."

"Right. He said something about women wearing cherry lip gloss and how unexpected things happen in the dark. I agreed. That's all I remember—again, all your fault."

He entered the bedroom and set her on the mattress with a gentle bounce. Leaning up on her elbows, her eyes glowing with arousal, she watched him undress, an exercise in torture that took him an interminable twenty seconds, a feat he could have accomplished in considerably less time if his damn hands had been steady.

Once undressed, he quickly rolled on a condom, then moved between her splayed thighs. Everything in him demanded a wild, fast ride and a quick, fiery finish. But those words *one last time* echoed through his mind, compelling him, forcing him to slow down. To savor when he ached to rush. To linger when he wanted nothing more than to bring a quick resolution to the desperate need clawing at him. To memorize every nuance, every touch, every look, every sound she made. One last time.

He entered her slowly, gritting his teeth against the intense pleasure of sinking into her tight, wet heat. Something flickered in her eyes, and she caught on to his shift in tempo. Was she thinking about this being their last time together?

"Give me your hands," he said, his voice hoarse.

She slipped her hands into his. Entwining their fingers, he settled their joined hands on either side of her head. With his weight braced on his forearms, he stroked her with long, deep thrusts, withdrawing nearly all the way from her body, then slowly burying himself again. Her gaze never left his as she moved to meet each stroke. Mesmerized, he watched her pleasure build then her orgasm overtake her, her back and neck arching, her body clenching his, her long purr of pleasure, her fingers gripping his. Dropping his face in the curve of her neck, he thrust a final time and his climax shuddered through him.

When he could move, he raised his head. And looked down into the most beautiful, chocolaty brown eyes he'd ever seen. And his inner voice reminded him, *That was the last time.*

14

MALLORY WALKED ADAM to the door, ignoring her clamoring inner voice that told her to lock the damn door, throw away the key and drag him back to her bedroom.

And it required all her willpower not to do just that. Especially after the exquisite way he'd just made love to her. Exquisite, yet poignant because she felt in his every stroke, his every look, a single word.

Goodbye.

He'd said it with his body. Now there were only the words. And then he'd be gone. And they'd both go on with their lives.

She reached for the door, but before she could turn the knob, his hand captured hers.

"It was an amazing night," he said softly.

She looked at his handsome face and her heart rolled over. "Yes, it was. Between last night and my prom, that's twice you've been my knight in shining armor. Better be careful or I'll get the impression you like me."

"I do like you. I always have."

Firmly telling herself not to place any significance

on his words—hell, he'd always liked steak and pota-toes, too—she smiled and said, "Same goes. Thanks for rescuing my wounded ego."

"The pleasure was all mine."

"Not *all* yours, I assure you." Now that the moment of goodbye was upon them, she felt the need to get it over with. To make a clean break. Because for reasons she didn't care to analyze, her heart felt as if an anvil were attached to it. Keeping her voice light, she said, "I hope you have a wonderful time in Europe."

A slight frown creased between his eyebrows. "Thanks. I'm, uh, really looking forward to it."

"Three months in Europe? Who wouldn't? I'm pea green with envy. What time does your flight leave to-morrow?"

"At 8:00 p.m. British Airways." He hesitated, then added, "I'll call you when I get back."

She went still, refusing to acknowledge the leap in her pulse. Before she could reply, he raised her hand and pressed a warm kiss to her palm. "I want to see you again, Mallory."

Every female cell in her body broke into a resound-ing chorus of "Happy Days Are Here Again," and she inwardly frowned. "I'd like that, Adam…"

"Uh-oh. I sense a *but* coming."

"It's just that three months is a long time. A lot could change between now and then."

"Such as?"

"Such as you might meet the love of your life in some piazza in Rome. Such as I might get swept off my feet by some real-estate magnate. I don't know. Anything could happen. The point is, I can't and won't put my life on hold for three months. And even if I did, what would be the point? Once you return from Europe, you're planning another long trip to some far-off place. You're going to move to who knows where, and I'm staying right here. We're basically in the same bad-timing place we were nine years ago—heading off in different directions."

For several long seconds he said nothing, just looked at her with a troubled expression. Then he cleared his throat and said, "I understand what you're saying, but I don't want to leave here thinking that we'll never see each other again. Won't speak to each other again. Won't still be…friends."

She hoped her smile didn't look as forced as it felt. "I don't want that, either. So why don't we leave it that you're welcome to call me in three months when you get back. Worst-case scenario is that we'll have a nice phone chat and catch up on each other's lives. Best case scenario is that maybe we'll end up spending another night together before you jet off to your next location or pack up your stuff and move to Hawaii."

Again he said nothing for several heartbeats and silence swelled between them. Then he finally jerked his head in a nod. "Fair enough. Agreed."

He then leaned forward and kissed her…a soft, gentle, tender kiss that ended far too soon and tasted irrevocably of goodbye. With a final quick smile, he left, closing the door behind him.

Reaching out, she laid her hand over the doorknob he'd just touched and remained standing there until she heard his car drive away. When the sound faded, she drew in a deep breath, straightened her spine, then turned toward the kitchen. No way was she going to mope. She had things to do, people to talk to, a career and life to think about. And the sooner she got to it, the quicker she'd put Adam from her thoughts.

Yeah, lots of luck with that, her inner voice sneered.

Shoving that pesky voice as far into the recesses of her mind as she could, she grabbed her cell phone and pushed the on button. She'd missed two calls, both this morning, one from her mother, one from Kellie.

Pulling up a bar stool, she sat at the counter and dialed her mom's number.

"I'm so glad you called, honey," Mom said. "Are you okay?"

No. "Yes. You're surviving the blackout all right?"

"Oh, yes. After I spoke to you last night, a dozen of us brought food and drinks and lawn chairs into the apartment-complex parking lot and we had an impromptu blackout party. Lots of fun. What did you end up doing?"

Mallory's gaze strayed to her breakfast table and an image of her and Adam and Rocky Road ice cream slammed into her. "I, uh, had a friend over."

"Kellie?"

"No. Do you remember Adam Clayton?"

"Of course. But you haven't seen him in years. Where did you meet up with him?"

Mallory related the G-rated version of the story, along with the news that she and Greg had broken up—but since a shot of mother sympathy was always welcome, she didn't skimp on those details.

"That jackass," Mom fumed. "I'm so sorry, Mallory."

"I'm fine, Mom, really. No broken heart, I promise."

"Well, I'm glad, although I know that it must have stung." She hesitated then asked, "So what was Adam like? Still handsome and charming?"

"Yes." *And sexy and sweet and funny and sexy.* "He was very…nice." Her gaze drifted again to the table. *Very nice indeed.*

"Well, just be careful about jumping into another relationship too soon, honey."

"Not jumping. But if the right guy comes along, believe me, it wouldn't be a rebound situation. Greg is already a distant memory."

"Good. How about lunch tomorrow? Are you free?"

"I am. Noon at my office?"

"I'll be there."

After saying goodbye, Mallory dialed Kellie's number. Her friend answered on the first ring.

"Has he left?" Kellie asked. "Are you alone?"

"Yes. Where are you?"

"My house. I can be on my way to your house within three minutes. I have a bottle of wine. It's warm, but hell, what can you expect with a power outage."

Mallory laughed. "Don't rush out. I have a few calls to make for work. I may have to show houses later today."

"You're killing me, you know that? You phone me last night and tell me you can't talk because Adam, your gorgeous former lover, is at your house, and now you tell me that you have to *work?* There's a phrase for that, Mal. It's called 'cruel and unusual punishment.' *Humph*. Just for that, I might not tell you the details about the gorgeous man I met at the beach yesterday… and who I'm seeing again this evening. Which means I'm only available for girlie chitchat until six o'clock."

"I want to hear everything. Let me make my calls and I'll phone you back."

After hanging up with Kellie, Mallory called the buyers and sellers she was supposed to see that afternoon. She tentatively rescheduled the appointments for early in the evening, in the hopes that the blackout would have ended by then. If not, then they agreed to reschedule for tomorrow. That done, she called Kellie back.

"I'm free for the next few hours, so come on over," she told her friend. "But forget the wine. I have possible appointments this evening. Got any diet soda?"

"Nope. But I have a container of Rocky Road in my freezer. It's probably half-melted but I'll bring it anyway."

Mallory squeezed her eyes shut. "Yippee."

KELLIE'S ARRIVAL AT NOON coincided with the power coming back on.

"How's that for timing?" Kellie asked with a grin, shoving her carton of half-melted Rocky Road in Mallory's freezer.

Since the temperature hovered near ninety, they closed the windows and Mallory cranked up the air conditioner.

"Ahhhhh," she said as the first blast of cold air hit her. "That feels so good."

"Quit hogging the AC, sit your butt down and tell me everything," Kellie demanded, commandeering the bar stool closest to the air conditioner.

"You first. Tell me about this guy you met at the beach."

"Why do I have to go first?"

Mallory waggled her eyebrows. "Saving the best for last."

Kellie's eyes widened, then without delay related her story of meeting one Mark Grainger at the concession line. "He was ahead of me and holding up the works because he'd ordered a half-dozen hot dogs and sodas and hadn't brought quite enough money. Turns out he was seventy-five cents short, so I handed him a dollar."

"In the interests of getting the line moving."

"Exactly. Plus, he had a great ass. When he turned around, the front view was just as great. Six-two, dirty blond hair, deep green eyes, killer smile *and* dimples. He was all kinds of polite gratitude and had the most amazing accent. Turns out he's from Australia and he's been in New York six months working for some international bank. He invited me to join his party, so I helped him carry his drinks. His party consisted of his two sisters, his brother and sister-in-law who were visiting from Down Under and one of Mark's male coworkers."

Mallory smiled. "I can see that you had a great time."

"*Great* is a gross understatement. I can't remember the last time I've laughed so much. They were all so nice—and they thought *my* accent was cool!" She shook her head and chuckled. "As for Mark…wow. Can you believe he insisted on paying me back my dollar? Said he couldn't let a 'lydee' pay for his food." She patted her chest. "Be still my heart. He's funny, smart, gorgeous, and so gentlemanly and polite. *And* he's employed. *And* he's heterosexual. *And* he's interested in me."

"He sounds terrific."

"Right. Which means there's got to be something horribly wrong with him."

Mallory laughed. "Maybe he's just a terrific guy. I know they're an endangered species, but there are still a few of them out there. Probably. So where were you when the lights went out?"

"We were all still at the beach. When the radio announcements advised people not to drive, we just stayed there."

"All night?"

"Yup. They had a cooler filled with drinks, bags of chips and pretzels, so we were set. Everybody else eventually fell asleep, but Mark and I stayed up the whole night talking. I swear, it felt like we'd known each other for years. Total clickage between us. And wow, does he know how to kiss." She heaved a dreamy sigh. "I'm telling you, Mal, this guy's totally knocked me silly. I've never experienced anything like this before. Every time he looked at me I felt positively woozy."

"Believe me, I know the feeling."

Kellie's gaze sharpened. "Well, since you haven't met Mark, you must be talking about Adam. Your turn to spill. Tell me everything."

There was no point in sugarcoating it—Kellie would see through that in a heartbeat. "The night was…amazing. *He* was amazing. Exactly as I remembered, only better. Charming, sweet, thoughtful. We talked and laughed, reminisced about the past—"

"And the sex was…?"

"Amazing."

"When are you seeing him again?"

The question brought a hollow pang to her midsection. "I don't know that I am."

"Ha-ha. When?"

"Seriously, I don't know that I am." She gave her a quick recap of how they'd left things. When she finished, Kellie shook her head.

"Mal, I understand you not wanting to put your life on hold, but it sounds like you and Adam have something special. Don't forget that eighty-eight percent, 'One Who Got Away' statistic."

"In this case, *away* is the operative word. Pretty hard to figure out if you have something special with an ocean between you. And I'm not about to sit around for three months while he's off discovering European women."

"He'll be back."

"And then he'll be gone again. Or moving to Hawaii, or somewhere else."

"Surely after three months in Europe he'll be all traveled out. Maybe you could persuade him not to go away again."

That brought her up short. And had her heart lurching. Persuade him not to go away again? "I…I don't know. I haven't had enough time to sit down and really think it through."

"Well, you need to. If hc's 'The One Who Got Away,' you don't want him to get away again. Chances are he found last night as amazing as you did. Which means that you'll be on his mind. Which means that when he gets home and sees you again, he might not be so anxious to go jetting off somewhere else or moving thousands of miles away. You said he wants to leave *Manhattan*—he didn't say he wanted to leave *New York*. Give the man a reason to want to stay. As for his trip, don't forget—absence makes the heart grow fonder."

"Don't forget—out of sight, out of mind."

"From what you told me, which was pretty stingy on the sexy details by the way, you will not be out of his mind."

"Three months is a long time."

"But it's not forever."

Mallory huffed out a laugh. "You have an answer for everything."

"Yes, I do. It's part of my charm." She batted her eyes. "Mark particularly liked it. He thought I was smart and savvy."

"You are."

"So are you."

Mallory managed a limp smile. "Thanks." But she didn't feel smart or savvy. Darn it, she felt like a deflated balloon, which was precisely what she didn't want to feel like. And it was all Adam's fault. Blowing back into her life with his sexy grin and blue eyes and everything that made him so irresistible, reigniting all the feelings she thought she'd buried, then breezing out again, leaving her reeling as if her emotions had been battered in a windstorm.

Well, he was gone and there was nothing she could do about that.

Or was there?

ADAM PACED AROUND Nick's kitchen, feeling like a large animal penned in a too-small cage.

"Dude, you've been here for ten minutes and done nothing but pace," Nick said. "Watching you is giving me a crick in my neck. Something's obviously bothering you, so why don't you just spit it out—preferably before I need a chiropractor."

Adam halted and a sheepish smile pulled at him. "Sorry."

Nick waved away his apology with his longneck beer bottle. "No problem. But my sleep deprivation is making my attention span about three minutes, so if you wanna talk—which I'm assuming you do since you're still here—you'd better get started."

Adam pulled in a deep breath then slowly exhaled. "I don't really know what to say because I'm not sure what's wrong."

"It's simple. If you know something's wrong, but you can't put your finger on what it is—"

"Exactly."

"Then it's a woman." Nick looked him up and down, his brows raising slightly when they hit the grass stains on the knees of his jeans. "Doesn't look like you got much sleep last night—something I can relate to, although I bet your lack of *z*'s had nothing to do with a crying baby."

"I spent the night with Mallory."

"Ah. Can't say I'm surprised. From the looks of you, it either went amazingly good or amazingly bad."

"There was nothing bad about it." Except that it had ended. And the way his damn insides had been knotted since he'd left her.

"For a guy who had an amazingly good night, you don't look too happy."

"I guess the problem is that I'd kinda like to have another amazingly good night." *Kinda?* He barely refrained from looking at the ceiling at that whopper of an understatement.

"I'm sure you'll find some gorgeous European women who'll be happy to oblige you."

"I meant with Mallory."

"Oh." Nick shrugged and took a pull on his beer. "So give her a call. You're not leaving till tomorrow."

"I thought about it, but..." He dragged his hands through his hair. Damn, he'd thought of little else.

"But you're needing some space."

"Yeah. I need to think—"

"And you can't think around her."

Adam stared at his bleary-eyed friend. "When the hell did you become clairvoyant?"

"I'm not. But I know the symptoms. I do have *some* experience with women—having married one and all. Besides, you're just easy to read."

"Really? Well, good. Tell me what I'm thinking because I have no freakin' idea and it's driving me nuts."

"Okay. This chick has you all fired up and you're bummed because you're hot for her, but the timing sucks because you're going away tomorrow."

"All true. But it's a little more complicated than that."

"Look, put it in perspective, man. You're going to *Europe*—another word for 'place where hot women dwell.' So enjoy yourself and call Mallory when you get back."

"She might not be around three months from now."

"She's falling off the face of the earth?"

"She might meet someone else while I'm gone."

"*You* might meet someone else while you're gone. As for Mallory, keep in touch with her while you're away to keep those home fires stoked. Phone her from Italy. E-mail her from France. Listen, chances are by the time you make it through those two countries you won't even remember Mallory's name."

Adam shook his head. "I don't think there's much chance of that."

"Oh. Well, then you're screwed."

"Meaning what?"

Nick held his hand to his ear. "What's that sound I hear? Oh, yeah. The death knell tolling for your bachelor days. Believe me, I know. I heard that same sound. Annie and I were married six months later."

Adam frowned. "I'm trying to be serious here."

"So am I. And you know what? That sound was the best thing that ever happened to me."

"But I'm not ready for that. I'm supposed to be resting. Relaxing. Living it up as a bachelor. Dating a slew of gorgeous women. Figuring out what I want to do with my life and where I want to do it."

"Good for you. Nobody's stopping you."

Adam nodded. "That's right."

"Your head's just messed up from a combination of too little sleep and too much sex."

"That's right."

"Totally feeling your pain on the too-little-sleep thing. No sympathy whatsoever on the too-much-sex thing."

"Understandable." Adam let out a long, slow breath. "Mallory would never move from Long Island."

"So the tiki bar in Hawaii would be out?"

"'Fraid so."

"Maybe Long Island needs a tiki bar."

"Maybe." He studied his friend for several long seconds. "How'd you know Annie was the one?"

Nick made a helpless gesture with his beer bottle. "I just…knew. I was happy when she was around and miserable when she wasn't. Every other woman just sort of faded away and I had no interest in being with anyone else. She was my best friend *and* I wanted to have sex with her—a great combination that I can only describe as the best of both worlds." He clapped his hand on Adam's shoulder. "It's what I'd wish for you. You think maybe you've found it?"

"I…don't know."

"This woman scares you."

"Yeah. She scared me nine years ago, too."

"And you let her get away. Might want to think about if you want to do the same thing again now. But hey, you've got the next three months to think about it."

"Right. Any advice?"

"About women? Yeah. After two years of marriage I can say with some authority that they want a guy who'll provide chocolate and who will shut up when they're talking. Never—and dude I can't stress this enough— *never* say anything that can in *any* way *ever* be construed as suggesting 'your ass looks big.' Other than that, I have no clue."

Adam raised his brows. "This is what you've come up with after two years of experience?"

"Believe me, there are guys who've been married twenty years who haven't figured out those pearls I just cast before you."

"I think I could have figured those little gems out on my own."

"I don't know. Women—they're tough to figure out." He nodded toward a photo of Annie holding Caroline. "But when you find the right one, they're worth the effort. It just boils down to deciding what you really want. What's going to make you happy."

He slapped Adam on the back and nudged him toward the door. "Now go home and pack so I can catch a catnap with my wife before our daughter wakes up. Have a great trip and touch base every once in a while, okay?"

Adam departed and spent the drive back to Manhattan and the entire night mulling over Nick's words. *It just boils down to deciding what you really want. What's going to make you happy.*

All he needed to do was decide.

And after hours of soul-searching, he finally knew.

When dawn broke over the city, staining the sky in

streaks of mauve and gold, he stood at the door of his
apartment, holding the handle of his wheeled suitcase.
With one last look around, he headed toward his car to
drive to the airport.

15

Monday, 11:55 a.m.

MALLORY GLANCED at her office wall clock and pretended that she wasn't thinking about Adam. Thank goodness her mother would be here in a few minutes. Lunch with Mom, telling her what she'd decided, would make the hours until she drove to the airport pass more quickly. She had a few things to say to Adam before his plane departed.

She hadn't slept much last night, but at least she'd done a lot of soul-searching and had finally figured out what she wanted. Now all she had to do was tell him.

As she was the only agent in the office at the moment, she plopped her purse on her desk and started digging for her keys to lock up when she went to lunch. She'd just felt them at the bottom of her bag when the bell above the glass door chimed.

Expecting to see her mother, she looked up from her purse with a wide smile.

And went perfectly still.

Adam stood just inside the doorway. Adam looking big and strong and gorgeous, wearing a navy pinstripe suit, white dress shirt and maroon paisley tie. Carrying a tremendous bouquet that had to contain at least three dozen pale lavender roses, the same delicate shade as the single bud he'd given her Saturday night.

Her heart performed an intricate maneuver and she swallowed to find her voice. "Hi."

"Hi, yourself." He walked toward her, his gaze steady on hers. Since her knees weren't feeling too well, she leaned her hips against her desk and strove to appear exactly what she wasn't—calm, cool and collected.

"What are you doing here?" she asked, proud of how smooth her voice sounded.

He stopped an arm's length away and handed her the flowers. "I wanted to give you these."

Their fingers touched when she took the tissue-wrapped bouquet, tingling awareness up her arm. "They're beautiful," she said, burying her face in the fragrant blooms. Then she lifted her head and smiled. "My birthday isn't for months."

"They're to thank you. For a beautiful night."

It took a great deal of effort not to heave out a gushy, feminine sigh. "In that case, I should have bought *you* flowers."

"And I wanted to see you again."

"How did you know where my office was?"

"I called your mom."

"My mom? *I* would have told you."

"And what sort of surprise would that have been? Besides, your mother and I had a great chat."

Her radar instantly quivered. A chat? With her mother? Her mother who knew Adam had spent the night during the blackout? Her mother who was an expert at extracting details before you even realized you'd imparted them?

"You'll be seeing her any minute," she said, trying not to sound wary. "I'm expecting her at noon." Her gaze drifted over his suit, purely in an observational sort of way. Certainly not in a "holy moly do you look incredible and my knees are sweating and I want you to kiss me so bad I think I'm drooling" sort of way. "You look more ready for a business meeting than a flight."

His eyes appeared to darken. "I'm hoping to have a business meeting."

"Before your plane departs? Boy, you have a tight schedule."

"Actually, I have lots of time." He lowered his chin then looked up at her, a boyish grin tugging at his lips.

Whew. Show her a woman who could resist that look and she'd show you a woman who...wasn't her.

"What?" she asked.

"I have a confession to make."

"I'm not a priest."

He made a great show of looking around the empty office. "Since there doesn't seem to be one available, I guess you'll have to do. I've commandeered your lunch appointment. Your mom won't be here any minute."

"How do you know?"

"When I told her that I was hoping to take you to lunch, she very graciously offered to reschedule. She'll call you later to find out what day this week is best for you."

"So now you're my lunch date?"

"If that's okay."

She was afraid even to consider how many ways it was okay. "Sure." Her lips twitched. "But I was kind of looking forward to girl chatting with Mom about the big sale at Victoria's Secret."

"I'm more than happy to talk lingerie. Bras and panties? I'm your man."

If only you were. "Well, as long as we're making confessions, I have one of my own." She drew a deep breath, then continued, "You said you wanted to see me again, and you would have. Even if you hadn't come here."

"Oh? How's that?"

"I'd planned to go to the airport to see you off this evening. Wish you bon voyage." *Tell you what I stayed up all night thinking about.*

Something flickered in his eyes. "I'm flattered."

"So where do you want to go for lunch?"

"How about your place?"

Vrrrooooom. Her libido, which had snapped to attention the instant she'd seen him, revved like a race car. And suddenly her mind clicked, like puzzle pieces falling into place. Dressed in a suit, business meeting, go to her place…

Was he trying to make her fantasy that they'd talked about come true?

Whew. Who the heck had lit the blast furnace in here?

Crossing her arms over her chest—for balance, as opposed to, say, grabbing him—she raised her brows. "So *lunch* is a secret code word for *nooner?*" *I hope, I hope, I hope.*

"No," he said, his expression perfectly serious with no hint of the heat that was scorching her. "There're just some things I'd like to discuss with you and I'd prefer to do so in private."

Her disappointment that he clearly wasn't thinking of her fantasy at all was replaced by curiosity. What did he want to discuss? Whatever it was, this worked out fine. She had her own list of things to tell him and she'd much rather do so in the privacy of her house as opposed to a crowded airport terminal. "I'm afraid my fridge is pretty bare."

"No problem. Lunch is in my car. Two take-out orders of 'the usual' from the Stardust Diner." He smiled. "For old times' sake."

"Wow. You sure know how to bribe a girl."

His smile widened. "That's what I'm hoping. So… do we have a date?"

"We have a date."

He stepped closer and cupped her face in his hands. Her breathing stuttered. Brushing his thumbs over her cheeks, he said softly, "Any chance I can kiss my date hello?"

Did she nod? She wanted to, but wasn't sure she could accomplish anything so complicated. She supposed she must have because he lowered his head and brushed his lips across hers. Softly, gently, in a way that made her entire body sigh with pleasure. And crave more.

Like a nooner.

He ended the kiss and Mallory had to press her tingling lips together to keep from asking him to kiss her again.

"Ready?" he asked.

He couldn't tell? Jeez, she was practically panting.

"You need help carrying your flowers?"

She blinked and sanity returned with a thump. Good grief, one kiss and he'd unplugged her circuits. Where the heck was the backup brain generator when you needed one? How could she hope to tell him everything she wanted to when he rendered her all but incoherent with a single kiss?

"Uh, no. I can manage, thanks." Grabbing her purse and her flowers, she walked briskly toward the door.

When they arrived at her house ten minutes later, Mallory immediately flicked on the AC unit to cool off the interior then headed into the kitchen where she reached for her favorite crystal vase.

"Table or snack bar?" he asked.

Their eyes met and for several seconds they stared at each other. A slide show of sensual images flicked through her mind and it was obvious from his heated expression that his thoughts were running along a similar vein.

"Snack bar," she said lightly.

He flashed a quick grin. "Chicken."

Yup. With a capital *C*. After adding water to the vase, she started arranging the fragrant blooms. "These are really lovely, Adam."

"Glad you like them. As I said, they remind me of you."

Her attention was distracted from her task when, from the corner of her eye, she saw him remove his jacket. Her hands faltered and her heart flipped over then thumped hard. Darting furtive glances at him, she watched him unpack the bag containing their lunch with one hand, while he loosened his tie and flicked open his top shirt button with the other.

This time her hands completely stilled and she swallowed. Oh, boy. He didn't say a word, didn't look at her, just continued unpacking the bag. If he rolled back his sleeves, she wasn't sure she'd be able to keep her hands off him.

She went back to arranging her roses, keeping one eye on him. After he finished setting out the lunch items, he met her gaze and slowly rolled back his shirtsleeves, revealing strong forearms dusted with dark hair.

Double *oh, boy.*

Giving herself a mental shake that helped not at all, she added the single bloom he'd given her to the arrangement then set the vase in the center of the table.

Sliding onto the bar stool, her gaze skimmed over that loosened tie, his rolled-back sleeves, and she nearly groaned. It was obvious he'd known all along exactly what he was doing. How she was supposed to concentrate on food, on what she wanted to tell him, when he looked so delicious she didn't know. He'd said he wanted to discuss something with her. Did he really? Or had he just said that to set up this little scenario for a round of goodbye sex? Either way, she wasn't about to rush things and say, *Let's just get naked.*

Maybe she'd suggest it after lunch.

Popping the top on her lunch container, she breathed in the mouthwatering combination of bacon cheeseburger and onion rings, glad to have something else to focus on besides him. Needing a hit of something cool, she first reached for her chocolate shake.

Silence swelled between them, a gap, which, due to the jitters bouncing through her, she felt compelled to fill. Deciding to play the game he'd set up, she asked, "What sort of business meeting do you have?"

"One concerning a career opportunity."

"Oh? Where? Doing what?"

"Here. On Long Island. Doing exactly what you mentioned. Buying fixer-uppers, doing the fixing up, then reselling them. Actually, this—" he waved his hand between them "—is the business meeting I was hoping to have. To discuss more details with you. To see if you'd be interested in showing me some houses."

Setting down her cup, she swiveled her stool to face him. "Are you serious?"

"Very. Are you interested in showing me houses?"

"I'd be happy to. When did you decide this?"

He pushed his untouched meal aside then turned his chair to face her. "Yesterday. Last night. All night. I did a lot of thinking."

"About your career?"

"About what I want. And what I don't want."

She had to press her lips together to keep from asking which category she fell into.

"Want to know what I decided?" he asked.

"If you want to tell me," she said with a studied nonchalance that deserved an Academy Award.

He reached out and took her hands, lightly entwining their fingers. Her heart fluttered at the contact, a sensation that intensified with the serious way he was looking at her. "I decided I want to be happy."

She blinked. "No offense, but that's sort of a no-brainer. Everyone wants to be happy."

"I agree. But I had to figure out what was going to make me happy. You see, I thought I knew. I thought that trekking around Europe, playing the field, scouting out tiki-bar sites was what I wanted. What would make me happy. Turns out I was wrong. Working with my hands, building things, fixing things—that makes me happy. Relaxes me. Investing money and seeing a return—that makes me happy. And it's also an area in which I have a lot of experience. The thought of buying a run-down house and fixing it up to resell makes me happy. In a stress-free way my doctor would certainly approve of. So I'm going to do it."

She squeezed his hands. "I think that's great, Adam. I have no doubt you'll be a smashing success."

"Thanks. But that's not all." He looked down at their joined hands, then raised his gaze back to hers. "*You* make me happy, Mallory. Being with you. Talking to you. Laughing with you. In bed, out of bed. Just looking at you makes me happy. It always has. From the first day I met you."

Her heart performed another series of flutters. Good grief, if this kept up *she* was going to have to make an appointment with a cardiologist. She supposed she should say something, preferably along the lines of *same here,* but her throat had swelled with emotion and the words wouldn't come.

"All that brings me to what I don't want. To what

won't make me happy. I don't want to put an ocean between us. I don't want to go three months without seeing you. The bottom line is that I let life separate us once before and it was a huge mistake. I'm not willing to let you get away again. I want to stay here. With you. There's something between us. Something really good and special and I want to see where it leads. Now. Not three months from now."

Her heart was pounding so hard she could hear the blood rushing in her ears. After clearing her throat to locate her voice, she managed to say, "But what about your trip?"

"I'm not going."

Good lord, she needed to sit down. Oh, wait. She was sitting down. Fine. She needed a stretcher. "You're giving up your dream—"

"No, I'm not. I'm just reworking it. The minute I stopped kidding myself about my ability to walk—or in this case fly—away from you, everything fell into place."

He rose and walked to the chair where he'd draped his suit jacket, then slipped an envelope from the inside pocket. After moving to stand in front of her, he held out the envelope.

"I stopped at the airport on my way here. I traded in my ticket for two open-ended vouchers. The thought of three months alone in Europe no longer holds any appeal. But visiting for a week or two—with you—does."

"You want me to go to Europe with you?"

"Yes. Whenever we can work it into our schedules."

"And you're sure about this?"

"Positive. You know that Olympic torch? That's nothing compared to what I'm carrying for you."

Adam reached out and clasped her shoulders, grimly noting that his hands weren't quite steady. His gaze searched her face, hoping for a clue to her thoughts, but the only thing he saw for certain was that she looked sort of…dazed. And stunned.

Hell, was that good or bad? Why didn't women come with instruction manuals? Clearing his throat, he said, "You're uncharacteristically quiet. Care to tell me what you're thinking?"

She blinked several times then looked at him through those big, melting, brown eyes that never failed to deliver a visceral impact.

"I was thinking that this is rather…ironic."

"Ironic? Is that…good? Because I gotta tell ya, *fabulous* or *terrific* were definitely more what I'd hoped for."

Not a trace of amusement flickered in her very serious gaze, and a very unpleasant knot gripped his stomach.

"Like you," she said softly, "I spent the entire night thinking. Soul-searching. Trying to pinpoint precisely what I wanted. And like you, I finally figured it out, and had planned to tell you tonight at the airport. Nine years ago, I made a mistake by not laying all my cards on the table and I don't want to make the same mistake now."

After drawing a breath, she continued, "Back then, you made me feel things I'd never dreamed possible. Things I haven't felt to that degree with anyone since. Things I'd basically given up on ever experiencing again. It was to the point where I almost believed I'd imagined I ever felt such…magic. But last night irrevocably proved it was no figment of my imagination."

She squeezed his hands, and he returned the gesture. "I find what you told me ironic because it so closely mirrors what I want to tell you. I want to see where that magic might lead, and I'm willing to do whatever's necessary to give it a chance."

"Meaning what?"

"I understand you wanting, needing to leave Manhattan, and if things show signs of working out between us, well, I wouldn't allow a house to come between us."

He went completely still. "Are you saying you'd sell your house? *Move?*"

"If it came to that, yes. I don't want to let life separate us again without knowing for sure what we might have together. Because I want, very much, to see where this might lead. Because you make me happy. In bed, out of bed. Just looking at you makes me happy. It always has. From the first day I met you."

Relief whooshed through him and he expelled a breath he hadn't even realized he'd held. A joy-filled laugh escaped him and he pulled her into his arms, hugging her close. "You know, right from day one of our friendship it was almost eerie how we were so often on the same wavelength."

"Obviously we still are," she said, smiling into his eyes.

"Thank God." Pulling her closer, he kissed her deeply, possessively, every cell in his body coming alive. When he'd satisfied his need to explore her luscious mouth, he left her lips to trail hungry kisses down her soft, fragrant throat.

She arched her neck, giving him better access, and moaned. Tunneling her fingers through his hair, she said in a smoky voice, "I'll give you five hours to cut that out."

"Five?"

"Okay, six hours. But not a minute more."

"Great." Bending his knees, he swooped her into his arms and headed swiftly down the hallway. "I vote we seal this occasion with that nooner fantasy of yours, brown-eyed girl."

Her smile could have lit a room during a blackout. "And there's that same-wavelength thing again."

Epilogue

Three months later…

MALLORY USED HER KEY to open the door of the fixer-upper Adam had recently purchased. This house was his second venture into his new career, the first having gone extremely well, netting him a nice profit when it had resold last week—also netting her a nice commission in the process.

Dust motes floated on the ribbons of late-afternoon sunlight pouring in the windows, and the rhythmic pop of a nail gun drifted up from the basement. A smile tugged at her lips. She knew exactly how he'd look—dusty, disheveled, gorgeous and sexy. How he managed to look gorgeous and sexy while being dusty and disheveled was one of those unfair advantages men just had over women. Her heart sped up with the knowledge that in less than one minute she'd be in his arms.

When they'd decided three months ago to see where their attraction might go, she'd been hopeful things would go well. She'd had no idea that things would go so extraordinarily well. Their relationship had bloomed into one of mutual respect and admiration. The awareness and sexual fire that smoldered between them continued to burn as hot as ever. She'd never known she could be this happy. This content. Or that she would fall this deeply in love. Again. With the same man. Only loving him even more now than the first time around.

Opening the basement door, she slowly descended the stairs. The nail-gun noise stopped, and Adam must have heard her footfalls because he came to the bottom of the stairs. Her heart sighed with pleasure at the sight of him.

"Hi, gorgeous," he said. He smiled up at her, but she noticed that the smile didn't quite reach his eyes.

"Funny, I was just about to say the same thing."

He raised his brows and looked down at his dust-streaked T-shirt and his old faded jeans that bore a multitude of smudges. "I'm a mess."

She stopped on the last step so that they were on eye level and, without the slightest thought to her black suit, looped her arms around his neck and pressed herself against him. "A gorgeous, sexy mess who'd better kiss me right now. Or else."

He leaned back, evading her kiss. "Or else what?"

"Or else I won't tell him about the handyman's special that was just listed on the market today."

"Done." He kissed her in that toe-curling, knee-weakening way of his that never failed to leave her breathless. But something felt…different. As if he were distracted. Her suspicion was confirmed when he leaned back and their gazes met. Normally when she greeted him, he looked at her with either warm amusement or blatant heat. Right now she saw neither. In fact, he suddenly looked very…unamused. Very serious.

"You okay?" she asked.

Something flashed in his eyes that she couldn't decipher other than to know it didn't reassure her. Neither did the fact that he released her and backed up a step.

"We need to talk," he said.

Uh-oh. Normally those words wouldn't have worried her, but there was something in his eyes, in his demeanor that edged real worry down her spine.

Reaching out, she rested her hand on his arm. "What's wrong, Adam?"

He raked a hand through his dusty hair. "I've been thinking about…us. And the thing is, Mallory…I'm not happy anymore."

Everything inside her seemed to stall. Her breath, her heart, her blood. An odd, numb sensation eased through her limbs and she had to lock her knees to keep them from shaking.

Not happy anymore? How was this possible? When had this happened? She wanted to ask him, but the words simply wouldn't come. Instead she just stared at him, his words echoing through her mind. When she was finally able to speak, all that came out was a whispered, "Not happy?"

He shook his head. "No. And I need to do something about it. That's why I brought you that." He jerked his head toward the far corner of the half-finished basement. Mallory turned and a puzzled frown pulled at her brows.

"A suitcase?" she murmured. His way of telling her to take a hike? Or maybe she'd misunderstood? A sliver of sunshine worked its way through the dark cloud his words had brought. Maybe the suitcase was filled with clothes—his way of telling her that he wanted to nail down a date for their trip to Europe? She latched on to that since the alternative rendered her incapable of breathing.

He walked to the corner, then wheeled the suitcase back, resting it next to her. "Open it," he said, crouching next to the piece of luggage, tugging gently on her hand.

Lowering herself next to him, she reached out with shaking hands and slowly unzipped the bag. Then drawing a bracing breath and offering up a quick prayer to whichever saint protected women in love, she opened the lid.

And stared.

At an entire suitcase filled with—

"Hershey's Kisses?" She stared in amazement at the little silver foil–wrapped drops. "There must be hundreds of them in here."

"Ten thousand," he said.

"Ten thousand?" She felt her eyes goggle and turned toward him to find him regarding her with that same serious expression. "You're giving me *ten thousand* Hershey's Chocolate Kisses?"

"Yes." Clasping her hands, he stood, drawing her to her feet. "And asking for ten thousand kisses from you in return. If you give me one every day, it will take you 27.39726 years to pay me back. At that point, I figure I'll fill up the suitcase with another ten thousand and we can start all over again."

Speechless, she slowly shifted her gaze from him down to the Chocolate-Kiss-stuffed suitcase, then back up to him. Her throat tightened and tears pushed behind her eyes, and she wasn't sure which she was going to do first—laugh or cry. Before she could figure it out, he gently took her face between his calloused palms.

"I love you, Mallory. And I'm not happy anymore just being your boyfriend. I want more. I want you. For the rest of my life. Will you marry me?"

She flung her arms around him and peppered his face, his jaw, with kisses, simultaneously laughing and crying. Then she leaned back and glared at him. "You scared me to death."

"*I* scared *you?*" he asked, brushing his thumbs over her wet cheeks. "You have any idea how nerve-racking it is to propose?"

"None. So let me try. Will you marry me?"

He hiked up his brows. "I asked you first."

"That means I can't ask you?"

"No, it means you're supposed to answer before you ask me."

"What if I say yes and you say no?"

He wrapped his arms around her and pulled her flush against him. "Not much chance of that, sweetheart."

"Okay, then yes. I'll marry you."

"Okay, then yes, I'll marry you, too." Laughing, he lifted her off her feet and spun her around until she was giggling and dizzy. "Looks like our timing finally worked out perfectly."

"Very perfectly."

Setting her back on her feet, he lowered his head and laid a searing, deep kiss on her that did nothing to make her less dizzy.

When the kiss ended, he said, "I already know what I want you to give me for a wedding gift."

"Gift? What makes you think you're going to get a gift?" She heaved an exaggerated sigh. "Good grief, we've been engaged for two minutes and already you want stuff."

"I want a set of boudoir photos of my beautiful, sexy wife."

"Ah. And you'll be the photographer?"

"Hell, yes. Like I'd let anyone else take the pictures."

"Seems fitting, especially since it was my trip to Picture This that reunited us." She smiled into his eyes and said, "How about we go buy a carton of Rocky Road and celebrate our engagement?"

He grinned and, lifting her off her feet, he started up the stairs. "And there's that same-wavelength thing again."

If you enjoyed what you just read,
then we've got an offer you can't resist!

Take 2 bestselling love stories FREE!
Plus get a FREE surprise gift!

Clip this page and mail it to Harlequin Reader Service®

IN U.S.A.	**IN CANADA**
3010 Walden Ave.	P.O. Box 609
P.O. Box 1867	Fort Erie, Ontario
Buffalo, N.Y. 14240-1867	L2A 5X3

YES! Please send me 2 free Harlequin® Blaze™ novels and my free surprise gift. After receiving them, if I don't wish to receive anymore, I can return the shipping statement marked cancel. If I don't cancel, I will receive 6 brand-new novels each month, before they're available in stores! In the U.S.A., bill me at the bargain price of $3.99 plus 25¢ shipping and handling per book and applicable sales tax, if any*. In Canada, bill me at the bargain price of $4.47 plus 25¢ shipping and handling per book and applicable taxes**. That's the complete price and a savings of at least 10% off the cover prices—what a great deal! I understand that accepting the 2 free books and gift places me under no obligation ever to buy any books. I can always return a shipment and cancel at any time. Even if I never buy another book from Harlequin, the 2 free books and gift are mine to keep forever.

151 HDN D7ZZ
351 HDN D72D

Name	(PLEASE PRINT)	
Address	Apt.#	
City	State/Prov.	Zip/Postal Code

Not valid to current Harlequin® Blaze™ subscribers.

Want to try two free books from another series?
Call 1-800-873-8635 or visit www.morefreebooks.com.

* Terms and prices subject to change without notice. Sales tax applicable in N.Y.
** Canadian residents will be charged applicable provincial taxes and GST.
   All orders subject to approval. Offer limited to one per household.
® and ™ are registered trademarks owned and used by the trademark owner and/or its licensee.

BLZ05   ©2005 Harlequin Enterprises Limited.

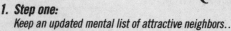

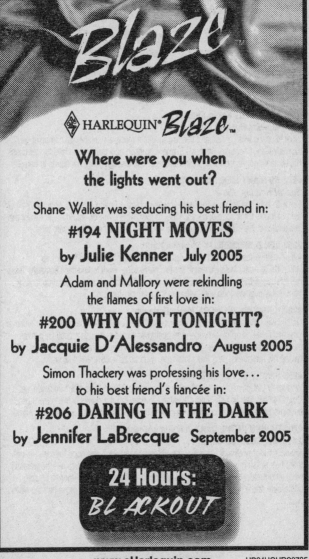

HARLEQUIN®

COMING NEXT MONTH

#201 UNZIPPED? Karen Kendall
The Man-Handlers, Bk. 2
What happens when a beautiful image consultant meets a stereotypical computer guy? Explosive sex, of course. Shannon Shane is stunned how quickly she falls for her client, Hal Underwood. As the hottie inside emerges, she just can't keep her hands to herself.

#202 SO MANY MEN... Dorie Graham
Sexual Healing, Bk. 2
Sex with Tess McClellan is the best experience Mason Davies has had. Apparently all of her old lovers think so, too, because they're everywhere. Mason would leave, except that he's addicted. He'll just have to convince her she'll always be satisfied with him!

#203 SEX & SENSIBILITY Shannon Hollis
After sensitive Tessa Nichols has a vision of a missing girl, she and former cop Griffin Knox—who falsely arrested her two years ago—work to find her. Ultimately, Tessa has to share with him every spicy, red-hot vision she has, and soon separating fantasy from reality beomes a job perk neither of them anticipated....

#204 HER BODY OF WORK Marie Donovan
Undercover DEA agent Marco Flores was used to expecting the unexpected. But he never dreamed he'd end up on the run—and posing as a model. A nude model! He'd taken the job to protect his brother, but he soon discovered there were undeniable perks. Like having his sculptress, sexy Rey Martinson, wind up as uncovered as he was...

#205 SIMPLY SEX Dawn Atkins
Who knew that guys using matchmakers were so hot? Kylie Falls didn't until she met Cole Sullivan. Too bad she's only his stand-in date. But the sparks between them beg to be explored in a sizzling, delicious fling. And they both know this is temporary...right?

#206 DARING IN THE DARK Jennifer LaBrecque
24 Hours: Blackout, Bk. 3
Simon Thackeray almost has it all—good looks, a good job and good friends. The only thing he's missing is the one woman he wants more than his next breath—the woman who, unfortunately, is engaged to his best friend. It looks hopeless—until a secret confession and a twenty-four-hour blackout give him the chance to prove he's the better man....

www.eHarlequin.com

HBCNM0805

Blaze™

Dear Reader,

We don't often think of twenty-four hours as being a long period of time. After all, it's just one day. But if we consider how drastically things can change in the mere blink of an eye, in a single heartbeat, it brings home the fact that the events that can occur during a twenty-four-hour period have the power to transform our lives. Especially if those events include the unexpected reappearance of The One Who Got Away. And even more so if those events are aided by a sudden blackout.

When former lovers Adam Clayton and Mallory Altman run into each other years later, neither initially believes that spending a mere twenty-four hours together will change the individual paths they've chosen for themselves. But throw in a heat wave, a blackout and a heap of overwhelming, sensually charged memories, and you have a recipe for a hot, dark excuse to relive some of those unforgettable, scorching past times. After all, it's only for twenty-four hours—what could be the harm? Adam and Mallory are about to find out.

I hope you enjoy their journey, and that it inspires you to turn out the lights and make some romantic memories of your own.

Enjoy,

Jacquie D'Alessandro

Books by Jacquie D'Alessandro

HARLEQUIN TEMPTATION
917—IN OVER HIS HEAD
954—A SURE THING?
999—WE'VE GOT TONIGHT?

"Believe it or not, it wasn't my intention to pounce on you the minute you walked in the door."

Adam's voice was husky with arousal.

Mallory looped her arms around his neck and rubbed her pelvis slowly against the hard bulge in his jeans. "Not to put too fine a point on it, but I think I'm the one who pounced on you."

His clever fingers walked her skirt up and his hands curved over her bare backside, lifting her higher against him. "I'm not complaining."

She moaned at the exquisite sensation. "Hmmmm. I can already see what will be my biggest weakness in dealing with you."

At his questioning look, she answered, "My knees. They aren't particularly steady."

"Then I guess we'll just have to lie down, won't we?" he said, grinning wickedly.

"I like the way you think," she said, slipping from his grasp. Then she entwined their fingers, about to lead him toward her bedroom…when the lights suddenly went out, plunging the room into total darkness.